DEFIANC

Beautiful Re:

Defiance Pattern

Beautiful Resistance, Volume 1

Sean-Michael Argo and Sarah Stone

Published by Sean-Michael Argo, 2023.

Also by Sean-Michael Argo

Beautiful Resistance
Defiance Pattern
Opposition Shift
Significant Contact

Extinction Fleet
Space Marine Ajax
Space Marine Loki
Space Marine Apocalypse

Necrospace
Salvage Marines

Starwing Elite
Attack Ships
Ghost Fleet
Alpha Lance

Standalone
War Machines
DinoMechs: Battle Force Jurassic

Also by Sarah Stone

By Sarah Stone
and
Sean-Michael Argo

Edited by TL Bland

1

Horatio's back was stuck to his chair. His spine felt fused to the worn leather through the fabric of his shirt. He scratched at the cable where it trailed out from the jack at the base of his skull. He had never gotten used to the feel of it plugged in.

No one else had ever mentioned it, but it seemed to Horatio that an odd taste lived in his mouth for the duration of each hack. It was like he'd licked a battery and couldn't get that acid sting off his tongue, no matter how many balance pills he popped.

The connection ignited and his fingers flew, faster than they ever could have while under his conscious control, the clacking sound of each digit against the keys taking over the small room he'd rented for the hack.

It was a squalid place in a bad neighborhood, but it was cheap and came with the kind of privacy that only slingers and junkies required. Horatio was of the former, self-taught, and as freelance as it got, but he had a few credits to spend and a ton more to earn, so it was worth what he'd paid. He liked it dark, the faint light of his screen, of the CodeSource display rolling in front of him, illuminating his surroundings like point-blank moonlight in the black room.

The Union Americana Mainframe was no joke, he thought to himself as his hands danced across the analog keyboard with speed and finesse, not that Horatio had expected anything less. He'd been hoping for a challenge, but he wasn't yet sure if this was within his capabilities, despite his self-assured act.

That was the curse of any slinger worth their rig, always caught between the opposing forces of the possible and the predictable, ever walking the lines of code in a dance that could end in a number of messy and potentially fatal ways.

The code flashed in front of him, the power of the jack allowing his mind to process the raw data while divorced from his conscious mind.

Some called it the monkey mind, the restless ego, the part of your brain that was always talking. The jack gave slingers a bypass, allowing them to apply the full force of their unleashed brain onto the task at hand. His eyes zeroed in on the flow of numbers and symbols, his focus narrowing. He made his way through the varying scrolls, searching for his opening, moving in and out of windows and programs, waiting for something promising to capture his attention.

Horatio, in fact, was a freelancer, in the game for a fast rip and the quickest cash he could make.

Waiting for something to exploit.

Far away, another slinger named Hayden Cole sat in front of his keyboard, a professional warrior jacked into his chosen field of battle. The computer had always been his weapon of choice—the one with which he could exact the most damage, as well as his most capable defense.

Most corporate slingers used the sleek VR boards that were all the rage these days, but Hayden preferred the click-clack of his analog keyboard. It was a tool of the old school, and he found that he lived for the sound of keys.

Several monitors projected in front of him, the information fed through the jack that rested perhaps an inch above the collar of the jacket he wore. No lags or surges plagued him. It was the best that money could buy, the most reliable technology Union Americana could afford.

If management couldn't force him to give up his analog rig, which was just as much a sign of criminality among the corporate elite as it was a sign of respect among the slinger subculture, the bosses were making damn sure he had the finest accessories.

His fingers punched the keyboard, chasing the flashing icons that had appeared within the reams of data. He had spotted them moments before, and they were unmistakable as anything but the presence of another hacker. Not well funded. Or at least, not as well funded as Hayden himself. Nobody went up against the Union Americana Mainframe who didn't have either a ton of cash to spend, an inflated sense of one's own skill, or a total death wish. Very few had all three, and whoever was poking around in there wasn't sitting on a pile of high-end gear. Even tech savants could push their freelance hardware only so far before they were outclassed by the guys with better funding, and today, that was Hayden Cole.

Hayden did not know the man, but he knew the type. He almost felt bad for whoever was on the other end because things were about to get ugly.

Horatio, his window found, kick-started a data rip to his stick drive and began to back out, navigating reversing the way he had come, his pulse thrumming hard beneath his skin, the way it always did when he was nearly done. He watched the data pour in, climb to halfway and then edge a little further. He had hustled for months to get a rig that could rip this hard, and Horatio was finally getting his payday.

Hayden watched closely as the freelancer swallowed the bait, pulling out just as his tagging program slotted into place. With an easy smirk, Hayden downloaded the data packet of information from his attacker. Everything, location, history, and target. There were more of these to fend off lately than he could count, and though each one was relatively easy, the sudden bulk of them was concerning. Freelancers with expensive street rigs who seemed to think they had nothing to lose. Maybe it was getting more desperate out there for normal folks than he realized.

He added a note and sent it along to his immediate supervisor, Overdog, who was in charge of his own crew of slingers charged with Union Americana's defense. His work done, Hayden sat back in his chair, fingers drumming absently on his knees as he scanned the code for another intruder. Hayden tried not to think about the nightmare that was about to descend on whoever that freelance slinger used to be.

Laine 2.0 stood atop a desert hilltop, the dirt dry and brown beneath her heavy boots. She moved through a series of fluid motions, the memories of a sword kata flowing through her body to make her movements seem as natural as they were deadly. The training was the closest she let herself come to truly relaxing. When a message pinged on her heads-up display, she didn't bother attempting to keep her features from twisting into annoyance. She stopped her movements mid-kata and browsed the attached file. Her last assignment had been particularly combat intensive, and the down time she had requested was only just beginning.

Laine scoffed. The kill order was for a free-lancer, stealing data from Americana, undoubtedly to sell it to one of their enemies. It was almost an insulting waste of her time. There would be no augmented security to break through, and a man this thoughtless would likely get himself killed by someone else soon enough. Likely as not, whatever organization he was doing the job for would off him afterward, tying up loose ends. This was a job for low rent mercs at best, barely even worth the attention of Union standard security. Putting this on the plate of an alpha-augment operative was so much overkill it positively reeked of ambition. Somebody lost something important, and they wanted it back with a bullet.

But an order was an order. If Laine didn't carry them out, regardless of how minuscule the task in comparison to her skill, she would not be nearly so well paid. Pass up a job, as they say, and soon there won't be any jobs. If one did not have jobs, one did not have purpose, and an alpha without a purpose was less than nothing. Close by, her weapons and her armor waited, lovers as eager for her familiar touch as she was theirs. Down time was for amateurs anyway.

Horatio was still grinning when he pulled out from the CodeSource trance, rubbing away the phantom sensation of the cable at the back of his neck. Once he was free from the jack, he destroyed it, along with the rest of his equipment, his foot cracking down on the keyboard he'd tossed to the floor. He uncorked a vial of acid and dowsed the pile of debris, and soon the whole thing was just a smoking heap of melted electronics.

He took a savage sort of joy in this bit, no matter the cost of the equipment in question. Some of the old hacks would hate him for desecrating such hallowed analog tech, but they were just tools to him, let the tech fetishist get all sentimental about this board or that board. Street rigs were made for hard use and little else, no point in getting all emotional about it. He would be paid handsomely enough for this that it was hardly a worry.

The young man knew that they had tagged him just as he downloaded the data, but that was out of his hands as well. He had security just for this sort of problem, no way was Horatio going down like a cheap street slinger.

When he was finished, the stick-drive was the only remnant of the hack. He slipped it into his breast pocket and gave it a pat, before pulling a cell phone from inside his jacket.

"Horatio, account number 5582874 Alpha Theta," he said, without waiting for an answering remark. He started out calmly enough but sped up in the midst of reciting his account number, growing jittery with the stick-drive in his pocket.

"I need three operators at my location, Priority One. Yes, I accept the additional fees."

He packed while he spoke, shoving the few things he'd brought with him that weren't smashed to bits into the simple black bag, some things you couldn't just smash, and zipped it shut.

He gave the room a quick look, eyes scanning over bare shelves, the chair he'd occupied, and a rickety desk that wobbled when he applied pressure to the wrong corner.

Horatio put one hand to his pocket, the weight of the stick-drive pulling it down with imagined heaviness, and pulled the thin curtain back from the room's only window. It was high enough on the wall that he almost needed to rise onto his toes to see from it. The street outside was quiet, just one man walking away from his current location and no moving cars on the pitted surface.

He heard the hum of the approaching vehicle before he saw it, nondescript as his clothing and his bag. The van drove close and nudged into the mouth of the alley that the door would open into. He stepped back, tapping one finger impatiently against the phone as he waited for an opportunity to speak once the line went hot.

"Takeda," he said at last, "It's Horatio. Yeah, I've got it, but they pinned me with a tag. No. I've got security picking me up now. Drop off location is the same, but come heavy, they might have an operative." He tapped the button to end the call and pocketed the phone. The bag was light on his shoulder, only the essentials. He'd pulled this sort of routine before, and now that he was out of CodeSource and away from whoever that corporate security slinger was, he was starting to feel better. Horatio paused to tug the curtain back into its place before he walked from the room, down the short, creaking hallway to the outer door.

The van was as close to the threshold as they could get it, but his head ducked down instinctively just the same, as though to hide his face from anyone watching. All street slingers were paranoid, not just him.

Horatio stepped out into the alleyway to the sight of three men, all in suits, his bodyguards, for as long as the journey lasted, and considering the retainer he put down, Horatio expected some change. One remained in the driver's seat, a second by the open door. The third covered him from the right, the side exposed to the mouth of the alley, for the short walk to the door of the van. The driver said something quietly, and though Horatio could not catch the words, he did see the slight glint of the earpiece he wore.

He stepped past the last man and settled himself into the seat.

Laine watched the man, her target, Horatio, from the upper floor of a nearby apartment, its owners seemingly gone for the day, or at least for the time being. She had sat on the bed while she waited, fingers grasping the white, lace-topped duvet, examining the strength of the fibers. It looked flimsy but did not pick or tear when she tugged at it. The walls of the room were blue, and she thought, perhaps, that it belonged to a child. But it was just a thought, and there were no toys scattered on the floor. The room looked unlived in, a guest room maybe.

She was about to stand, to run through the motions of her sword-kata again, when a black van made its way into the alley she'd been staring at.

It moved slowly. The buildings to either side pressed close enough to make the entrance narrow. She saw the curtains, an ugly green, flick closed. There was more than enough time to shoulder her gun, looking through the scope for a better view. It showed her the area in close up slices, without the rest of the world attached.

Her target had the same dark hair she'd viewed in his file, with a messy look that said he ran his fingers through it often, perhaps with increasing frequency when events moved quickly. As she watched, he did it again. She could have shot him then, though her window was nearly nonexistent before there were suited men in her line of sight. It was best to wait in this case. Best to learn something from following.

The door shut behind the target, closing him in behind glass that was tinted and likely bulletproof besides. Her heads-up display scanned over the license plate as she looked at it, pinged in acknowledgment at the string of numbers, and sent them to Overdog. The number was also added to a file at the forefront of her heads-up, saved with a string of other license plates, phone numbers, and addresses. Similar information gained the same way, that would perhaps be useful more than once, or at least point to valuable correlations.

A trace notification chimed near her ear. Headquarters knew. All was set.

It was not a long VTOL flight from the desert and Laine always traveled with full kit. Following the target was not difficult.

Horatio shifted in the van. The seats were too hard, his shoulders aching when he leaned against them despite the short drive. He blamed his still tense muscles on the recent, more or less successful hack, and tried to forgive the uncomfortable vehicle. He was grateful when it pulled into a warehouse after several minutes of driving over the pothole littered streets.

In the wealthy neighborhoods and the commerce districts the streets were kept pristine by maintenance drones, but out here, in the sprawl, there wasn't much in the way of well-maintained infrastructure. It was all falling apart, and everyone knew it, even if they just went about their day to day in spite of that grinding truth. Inside, the only light came through a string of high windows to one side, leaving everything within in shadow, gray, motes of dust drifting listlessly through the air.

Takeda himself waited near the parking area, his back unnaturally straight, his gaze locked on the van as it rolled slowly through the warehouse.

A cyber samurai stood with him, scanning the area with far more efficiency than Horatio's three rented bodyguards would have been able to do together. The cybernetics made the samurai's eyes look too bright, like the reflection of an animal in headlights. It only compounded Horatio's growing uneasiness. That was a beta-augment operative, and just having one around would cost more than what Horatio had originally thought the hack was worth. Maybe he should have asked for more.

The van slowed to a stop in the parking area, a bit closer to Takeda than Horatio had hoped to step out. He'd had his fingers crossed for a moment to compose himself, to practice the explanation regarding the tag in his head, but now, from this close, stalling would look like nothing but stalling. He had no choice but step out behind his bodyguards after two heartbeats had passed.

Laine watched the zoomed in view through her scope, eyes narrowed behind mirrored shades, her armor a comfortable weight on her muscular, yet impossibly lithe body. She could see well enough to watch the apprehension play across her target's face, the slightest bit of worry before one of his bodyguards opened his door and waited for him to step out.

She waited until all three of them were free of the cage of the car, before following Horatio and the guard beside him with her scope. They stopped, as she expected them too, a few scant feet away from Takeda and the cyber samurai, speaking from a distance. She watched her target's feet shifting on the dusty concrete floor. Poor kid was so far out of his depth he didn't realize the water was already over his head.

She pulled the trigger, the crosshairs zeroed on the guard closest to her target. Non-augmented according to her scope, so she aimed for the center of mass and squeezed the trigger to send a high-velocity round shrieking through the air.

The shot was loud to the others, ringing and painful, but small implants in her ears prevented the noise from damaging her hearing, stifling it temporarily.

The guard's chest exploded from the impact of the heavy round, splattering Horatio with blood. Takeda snapped forward and grabbed the slinger, hauling him away. The samurai trailed behind the pair, eyes still scanning, his hand straying to the handle of an edged weapon hanging from his hip. He was looking for her, but his eyes only checked the obvious places. The operative was at the opposite side of the warehouse, in the shadows to the back, where she had dropped down from the darkest of the high windows moments before.

Laine moved her scope with absent skill, locking on to the two remaining suited bodyguards. She dropped first one and then the next, her movements methodical to the point of mechanical before she shouldered her gun and stood.

She barely moved above a steady, quick paced walk to catch them, knowing their fear would likely make their flight messy, loud, easy to follow. If she ran, she risked being out of breath for the next long shot, and half the trick to aiming was in the way she held herself.

Laine walked past the blood puddled on the floor, shifting into strange shapes as the cracks in the concrete directed its flow.

It struck her as a thing of beauty worth capturing, and so she blinked, activating the ocular screenshot feature of her enhanced eyes to record the image in perfect detail. There were hundreds of such images stored in her private drives and had she run after the target she might have missed it. She was not an android, Laine told herself with some intensity, and there was more to this than simple efficiency.

Takeda was nearly dragging Horatio, making it hard to keep up with him. Horatio's feet felt out-of-synch with the other man's and he stumbled several times before they came to a stop in a hallway.

He leaned against the wall with one shoulder, heart and lungs in overdrive as he swiped at the blood on the side of his face. His collar and shoulder were wet with it, but he was sure that the bullet had missed him. It had been meant for the bodyguard and not him.

They should have still been running. Horatio was sure of that. The shooter couldn't be far behind them, and his ears were still ringing from the shot.

Horatio looked up at Takeda, straight into the mouth of a gun.

He pushed himself back, further into the wall, so hard that he could feel the knobs of his spine against the cold metal.

Takeda's fingers found his pocket, fished out the stick-drive with ease. The gun never lowered.

"The deal has changed, Mr. Horatio. The cost of this altercation has pushed your fee into the negative, and thus, you are indebted to us."

The samurai, until then a quiet presence behind Takeda's left shoulder, stepped forward.

Horatio saw movement, felt the blunt, heavy hit of something in his gut, and fell gasping to the floor, his lungs floundering. Two sets of footsteps raced away, one moved forward. The boots were heavy, but the step was light. Coughing, he pushed himself up.

Laine, entering through the same door the others had come through, casually shouldered her rifle and shot Horatio in the chest.

The target fell, breathed out and died.

So much for freelance street slingers, thought Laine as she stepped over the body and moved down the hall. He had been young enough that some might call his execution a tragedy, though no such judgment would come from Union Americana. He sliced the system and he paid the price. It was the way of the Union to balance that equation, and it was Laine's way to be the instrument by which that balance was achieved.

It was not a long hallway, and there was only one door that waited at its end. Her heads-up display, had she needed it, could have shown her their footprints laid out in front of her as a map on the floor, but pulling it up again was a waste this close to the end of the line.

They hadn't even bothered to close the door behind them.

Outside, Takeda and the samurai were both focused on the car, the way she often only saw her target through the scope of her gun. Tunnel vision was common amongst humans who were in a crisis situation, and this was certainly that. They were outclassed and they knew it, though in the fixation upon their flight they neglected to consider fighting as an option. By doing so, it was she who chose the time and the place, having not so gently pushed her quarry ahead of her onto a suitable dying ground.

She fired off a shot at Takeda, hastily aimed more by instinct than her augments, though she must have telegraphed her movement in her casual confidence because the samurai shoved Takeda to the side just as the operative squeezed her trigger.

The bullet drilled through Takeda's shoulder, exiting messily through the other side of his body and forcing Takeda to stagger. To his credit, the man remained on his feet, despite his lack of augmentation and the grievous wound dealt to him.

Well done, Yakuza, thought Laine as she intentionally slung her rifle and placed a gloved hand on the hilt of her vorpal sword. Management would have a field day with this, as it was a serious breach of protocol. Laine smiled to herself, they should know her well enough to have seen this coming.

She kept walking. Laine thumbed the activation stud on the hilt of her weapon and a telescoping blade extended and locked itself into place. The samurai produced his own blade, a katana that had been modified with an atomic edge capable of cutting through industrial strength augments as easily as it would flesh, and charged. Laine was more than ready to meet him.

Her heads-up display rushed to guide her strikes, picking up on micro-tensions in his musculature that allowed Laine to predict and counter his movements. His attacks were easy to block thanks to state of the art cyberware, Laine's mind calculating and recalibrating her body more swiftly than the samurai's. She was faster than he could ever hope to be, her brain already ten moves ahead. The samurai swung his blade in a wide arc that would have sliced into her side had she missed the parry. Laine realized that while the man had been augmented for strength and resiliency, perhaps even had parts of his brain adjusted for loyalty, there was little he could do against her so long as he thought too hard about it.

Any fool could swing a sword, and anyone could become a master of the blade with enough training or upgrades, yet it was only with no-mind that one could hope to win with consistency. The woman allowed her augmentations to feed her data and silenced her conscious mind, allowing her ego and her assumptions about the outcome to dissolve into the data stream from her augments. The cyberware rode Laine into battle, her ego given over to the machine's lightning fast calculations.

Perhaps, had the samurai also achieved a similar state, free of his conscious mind, he could have beaten her. To act without thinking, to be as pure as the kata, was the only way to even have a hope of beating the machine.

Laine sidestepped another swipe of the samurai's blade, driving her own into his throat, through the windpipe and the spine in one stroke. The samurai's body sounded hollow as it hit the ground, sword clanking against the pavement, all of it recorded by Laine's auditory enhancements. The bodies always sounded hollow to her ears, as they died, no matter how augmented or not they might be. Often, she would listen to their final moments over and over, as if hoping to divine the exact moment life left limb and spark died in the wire.

Her eyes tracked the progress of Takeda to the car, one hand pressed tight to the wound on his shoulder. He made a pained noise, collapsing against one side of the vehicle, where he began uploading the data from a handset. Laine adjusted the grip on her sword and walked toward him. She caught him trying to stand on the opposite side of the car, reaching for the door handle.

He fell when she reached him, trying to crawl away, his blood slick beneath him, one side painted red. Seeing her nearly upon him, his movements stuttered to a halt. He looked at her with defiance, which was more bravery than most would show in her presence, such was the hallmark of the hard men who became field operatives for the Yakuza.

She reached out to snatch the handset from his faltering grip. Whoever had hired these gangsters had paid a high price for high caliber henchmen, much good it had done them.

"You're too late, cyborg." Takeda spat, his voice wavering with pain and blood loss, though the snarl on his face was iron clad. "We know. The game is afoot."

She wasted no breath on a response. Parlay wasn't her job. Her sword impaled him, making red froth at his lips. Laine pulled her sword free as his last breath shuttered out from his lungs, and cleaned the blood from the metal before she replaced it in her sheath.

"Critical failure," she spoke, looking down at the body propped against the car and back to the samurai's fallen sword, knowing she was going to be severely chastised for taking the time to duel instead of simply shooting everyone. "Partial data loss."

Hayden Cole remained in the chair in which he'd begun the day. He could have paid for a better one, perhaps, something leather and comfortable that did not make his back ache. But then he risked falling asleep. Aside from that, he did not expect to be in one place for very long. Much of his work was remote to some degree, but that didn't stop Union Americana from dragging him along each time a new source of power or wealth piqued their interest. It was safer, he knew, to do his work from a secure site, but that did not stop him from occasionally tiring of the movement. He wanted, someday, to have a permanent space of his own.

The attacks from their rivals, E Bloc and Asia Prime, had been growing more frequent and more persistent, which usually proceeded a revelation of some sort. A move to a new site with something else that needed his expertise or his protection. Another possible energy source. Another network that either needed attacking or defending. Another path to profit for his masters to carve out of the post-war civilization that has risen from the ashes.

The war that only in its aftermath had been ruled the 3rd World War, had been long and bloody, and he had missed most of it, having been too young to see more than the news reports that surrounded it.

The world had been a powder keg, just waiting for a spark to shake the nations. It had been a combination of factors, he had learned, not enough resources and too much religion. Nearly every country, in some manner, played their part in the carnage, and when the dust had settled, three conglomerates emerged. Union Americana, the ones who wrote his paycheck. E-bloc, the combination of every small European country into one vast nation, and Asia Prime, a monster of the same make as all the rest, but Hayden often worried that their current supply of resources far eclipsed that of his own group.

He stood, stretched, felt something in his back pop and slot back into the correct alignment. Damn chair. He fiddled with the jack at the back of his neck, thinking about removing it, but on most occasions, it was scarcely an hour or two before he was tasked with something else that required it. Most nights, he fell asleep with it still jutting from his neck, head turned to one side to accommodate the awkward placement.

Ah, the glamorous life of a world class slinger.

A flash in the corner of his eye had his display rising up to greet him. A meeting had been called. He looked around the sparse, office-like room, and blew a huff of air through his nose. Duty called. Again.

"Down time is for amateurs," huffed Hayden as he prepared himself.

2

Hayden was early, but in his defense, he was already closer than the other personnel that were likely be called. There were benefits to living in the mega-city of New Los Angeles.

There was a row of chairs set neatly in front of a long metal table. The Union Americana logo hovered in front of a white wall that the chairs faced, the three-dimensional hologram rotating in such a way that it made Hayden think of a giant eye that watched over everything.

He took a seat near one end of the table and sat back. He was considering pulling up his display, maybe bring up one of the old Atari games those tech archaeologists had unearthed and put on the black market and had half moved to do so when the door opened.

A young woman strolled into the room, wearing a casual shirt and tight jeans. Her head was partially shaved on one side, the longer locks on the other side dyed a bright blue.

She nodded when she saw him. "Hey. You're Hayden Cole. I'm Nibiru, you know, like the planet."

"Nice to meet you," he said reflexively, and then added, "Haven't run across that handle yet, at least on Overdog's crew. You a slinger?"

She shook her head and brushed her hair aside to show that she only had one set of jacks for CodeSource, not the double set that slingers had which granted their minds access to MassNet, the exclusive dominion of only the most hardcore of slingers. "The technical title is hardware specialist, or solid systems technician, or engineer if you want to cover all the bases. But I know my way around CodeSource if the need should arise."

"I don't usually need back-up," he replied bluntly. Her expression hardened and he added, with an awkward attempt at warmth, "But it's, um, appreciated."

She sat down in the chair closest to him. "You're kind of an asshole. In case you didn't know."

He couldn't help but let his lips tug upward in response. That was the way of things for folks like him, most social graces lost in the data cascade. If he wasn't naturally a handsome guy with cash to spend he probably wouldn't even have friends.

Well, at least he was a generous tipper. "Yeah. I'm aware."

Laine was next to arrive, Captain Mitchell striding in after her.

Laine walked with the same careful precision with which she did everything else. It unnerved some people, Hayden knew, but the two of them had worked the same ops enough times that the sight of her brought nothing but a sense of security. She was a good person to have on one's side and a bad one to be up against. Not much for conversation or what one might consider the usual banter between co-workers, but if she was on the team he figured this was a heavy job and was glad to see her.

Union Americana had fronted the cost for the technological upgrades to her skeletal and nervous systems, along with heaps of cybernetics which made her as much of a killing machine as a human being could be and still be considered mostly human.

She was deadly accurate with any sort of gun, but Hayden knew from their many and varied jobs together that she preferred a sword and a fearsome opponent, living for the rush of a good fight rather than an expedient execution. It made her something of a wild card as far as management was concerned, but she was bought and paid for and always got the job done. Her loyalty though was not an easy thing to win, and she would do anything that Americana asked, even if it didn't quite fit her definition of a challenge.

Captain Mitchell was a familiar sight as well, one of the head military operators who ran the security platoons for the corporation. Normally, his job consisted of providing field support to Laine and close protection to Hayden while their work was carried out. He was career military, a militia man for one of the upstart republics before the company bought him up, and his attitude still said so. He sat at the other end of the table but gave Hayden his usual stern (though good-natured) nod as he did so.

Laine took the seat on his other side, perhaps an inch taller than Hayden even while sitting. She sat up straight and on anyone else the posture would have looked stiff, but on her, it simply looked right. Like the way, Mitchell still stood with shoulders back. This was an interesting lineup, Hayden thought with some degree of excitement, a killer, a military man, a slinger, and an engineer.

Hayden rocked back in his chair impatiently, gripping the table's edge. He looked at Laine's armor, black with accents of red, well-made and well looked after. Wearing it was not unusual, even outside of a job. All the alpha augments were like that, treating their battle dress like it was a kind of second skin. But the dried specks of red along the arm closest to Hayden were not expected.

"No time to freshen up?" he asked.

She nodded, swept her light hair back with one hand. "They called in a strike on your freelancer."

"I'm gonna go ahead and guess it wasn't the highlight of your career." Hayden smirked outwardly, though he had to admit that there was a pang of guilt that ran through him, which came as a surprise. Was he getting soft? Nah, couldn't be, just impressed by the pluck of whoever that dead man was.

Laine's lip twitched, the closest she ever came to full on smiling. He knew her well enough to look into her eyes and see humor hiding there, despite her deadly reputation. Honestly, it was these hints of almost a real personality that creeped him out more than her capacity for extreme violence. Everyone thought of the alpha augments as killing machines, if they were honest with themselves, and it always rattled the mind a bit when forced to acknowledge that they were still people underneath all that cyberware.

"It wasn't the most fun I've had," she replied. She gave him a brief run-down of the job, while they waited, telling him about the layout of the warehouse and the target's frantic meeting with Takeda, a member on the lower rungs of a Yakuza gang known to have deep connections with various branches of Asia Prime. When the story was told, the room still held only the four of them, empty of the man in charge.

Captain Mitchell sat with his hands folded on the table in front of him, staring at the rotating logo on the screen in silent thought. Nibiru had grown impatient enough to lift her heads-up display and was staring at something that Hayden couldn't see. Probably a video of some sort, or perhaps, though he doubted it, something related to the upcoming job.

Hayden looked to Laine again. "He's late."

"Power play," responded Laine, "Surprised?"

"No," he answered.

Bascilica chose that moment to enter the room.

Yep, power play.

He was a fairly young man to be where he was in the company, not far from Hayden's own age. His hair was so dark it was almost black and he was always smirking.

As Hayden watched, he walked steadily to the front of the room and stood in the center of the screen, obscuring the view of the still slowly spinning logo. Hayden nudged Nibiru, who gave him a half-smile in return and turned her gaze on Bascilica, watching him with interest, as though forming a profile of his behavior in her mind.

Hayden already knew there would be no apology for the wait. He hadn't worked under the man for an especially long time, but so far, his behavior had not varied. He would have been surprised if the word 'sorry' even existed in the man's vocabulary.

Normally, he liked to go on a spiel of some sort beforehand, but for whatever reason, he wasted no time. He swept his hand through the holographic image of the logo and soon had it replaced with a rendering of an island. The model was 3-D and detailed, the climate obviously tropical from the bright green of the foliage and the blue of the surrounding water.

After a moment of staring at the shape, Hayden was able to recognize it as a series of island chains commonly known as the Philippines. There was a dot highlighted far to the left, the capital city.

"This," Bascilica said simply, "Is your mission site."

Manila, read the name above the dot.

"This is what you need to know."

Bascilica had a voice made for speeches, whether given in boardrooms or stadiums, and he did not disappoint. Hayden had wondered before if he wrote them out beforehand and practiced them in his living room. Or maybe he paid someone to write them for him, had the words scrolling in front of his eyes via the high-tech glasses he wore, reading them out as they came. The thought made the man seem a great deal less intimidating. He would have liked to share the thought with Laine. Loyalty aside, he was sure the joke would win another slice of a smile.

"We've traced the energy source to here," Bascilica pointed to the center of the image, and smiled at his audience. "It's a pulse, if you will, that emanates from this chain of islands, and now that the frequency of that pulse has been lifted by our competitors, there isn't much time to get a proper research and development team on this. If we succeed in harnessing it, it would be powerful enough to virtually replace our current resources. No more fossil fuels."

Bascilica lifted his hands and spread his fingers, speaking as though he was giving a pitch to an audience of investors, either forgetting or simply not caring that the room's occupants were already on the payroll. Even Nibiru, unfamiliar though she was to the slinger, would not have been brought on board one of Bascilica's ops without having earned her place at that table.

Say what you will about this guy's style, thought Hayden, as he listened, he was a player of the great corporate game and the word milk run was not in his vocabulary.

"The local government has been, shall we say, persuaded, to look the other way, not that we should expect anything less of our negotiators here at Union Americana." He paused, but when applause was not forthcoming, plunged ahead. "Though this is good for our mission, it does mean that we can expect no interference on their part should we meet opposition. And we almost certainly will.

"Because of the leak we have recently experienced, our rivals, E-bloc, and Asia Prime are likely already aware of the nature of the situation. We can assume that they are in the midst of gathering their own teams, and we have intelligence that states E-Bloc already has boots on the ground that have been clashing with local interests."

He paused, looked seriously at the table before him for the first time since he began to speak.

"The importance of the potential profits and overall economic change cannot be overstated, but there just isn't time to move patiently with an R&D approach, so I'm admitting right now that we are rushing in because we have to in order to beat the competition. As a result, you'll be making this up as you go, which is why you see the faces you do at this table.

"We'd go in there with fighter jets and tanks if there weren't already so many players on the board. So, we do this clandestine, with a small team of our best operatives. The performance bonuses alone could retire you into luxury but drop the ball on this one and we all disappear forever. Do you understand?" His tone, briefly, took on a serious inflection.

He received a series of scattered nods for his answer but seemed satisfied enough. Captain Mitchell was the only one who bothered with vocalizing his assent.

"Though the local government is aware of our involvement in the region, the specifics are not known, and it is important for each of you to remember that this is still a covert operation," he said, looking straight at Laine as he spoke.

Hayden nearly chuckled. All of their work for Americana was covert. Why should this be any different? He, too, looked at Laine, but in mock seriousness. She studiously ignored him as well as Captain Mitchell. Now that an executive was in the room, he understood the need for her loyalty to be projected. A laugh, however harmless, had the potential to call her unwavering loyalty to Bascilica into question.

"There will likely be opposition in several areas, but we expect the majority of the harassment from E-Bloc to come from the city. We are currently aware of only one of the operations centers, based somewhere here." A map of the city rose as he spoke, and Bascilica waved his finger at a circled section, shaded red. "By the time you all arrive, they may have altered their position, but we'll send any updates to you as soon as we have confirmation of their accuracy. Drone recon is extremely limited, as Asia Prime and E-Bloc both have already erected baffle systems, and until we have Nibiru there with her smaller models we won't have much to go on. We are late to the party, so will have some catching up to do."

Bascilica pulled up yet another image with a flick of his wrist, this showcasing a mapped-out area of jungle. "Captain Mitchell and Laine, this is for you two specifically. We'll be in the unique position of worrying about physical security from local resistance forces, in addition to Asia Prime and E-Bloc operatives."

The hologram switched to a video image, slightly on the grainy side, even with Union Americana's technology, which told Hayden that the footage had come from an older security camera. When the movement coincided with footsteps and the static sound of even breathing reached his ears, he revised his theory. It was one of the body cameras that most soldiers wore, though he had no way of knowing if it had been uploaded by a platoon of their own, or if it was from a soldier of Asia Prime or E-Bloc, obtained through other means.

The picture showed a street, little cared for, littered with potholes. A car parked to one side, parallel to the road, one of the older models that ran on pure gasoline instead of the hybrids everyone in the Union who could afford their own vehicle used.

The other side, when the camera turned, was all trees—the vibrant green muted by the poor-quality picture, the individual plants blurring together at the jolting footsteps. The walking halted suddenly at the sound of footsteps squelching on the wet ground.

Beside him, Laine now leaned forward in interest. It looked close to twilight, but aside from the camera's drawbacks, the picture was clear enough. Shapes moved in the forest, a group of people weaving between the trees.

The soldier turned, revealing several more men, at his back. Now that their clothing was visible, Hayden could recognize them easily as E-Bloc men.

There was a quiet chorus of whispered expletives, followed by one delayed, *the fuck was that?* Despite the unknown, the soldiers moved forward. One close to the back, far enough away that his speech came through garbled, could be heard speaking, asking for permission to investigate. The answer was immediate, but completely unintelligible, as the lead man was still moving forward, taking their current point of view along with him. The shadows flashed again, this time closer, and Hayden saw one of the figures run several feet up the side of a tree before using it as a springboard to leap forward. And then back into shadow.

Their guns now free from their shoulders, the soldiers moved into the jungle. The camera switched over to nothing but static, the jarring sound of white noise coming in too loud in the small room.

Bascilica let it play, looking at them eagerly.

Hayden decided to speak if only to get the man to turn the feed off. "What the hell was that?" he asked.

Immediately, he was gratified by the sudden silence of the display reverting to a still of the last unknown figure. It was hard for Hayden to make out more than the shape of him, but he thought that its eyes had a peculiar brightness.

"Those," Bascilica answered, with all the glee of a kid about a launch into their favorite campfire story, "Are the Akiaten."

Even Laine's face was perplexed. "The Akiaten," she echoed, committing the word to memory.

"They are...'" Bascilica considered his words carefully for a moment before continuing. Apparently, this part of the speech was unscripted, something that suddenly made Hayden rather nervous. This truly was uncharted territory.

"A very odd group of locals, a resistance of sorts, who have been giving E-Bloc quite a bit of trouble. Our own base has only just been established, so we haven't had too many issues ourselves, but according to various sources, their attacks have been growing more coordinated, and they seem to be rising in numbers as well."

That didn't answer the question, but Bascilica at least had the presence of mind to acknowledge this.

"They are a part of a particular group who seem to believe that the energy source we're after is sacred and allows them certain...abilities. We know that they are adept at free-running, as you saw, but there are other, frankly ridiculous stories being passed around among the locals. Our recon efforts have yielded very little in the way of verifiable data, mostly just coming up with rumors about myths and folklore.

"We are also aware that they have their own group of slingers, resisting all attempts by E-Bloc and Asia Prime to establish a fully operational network. The upside to this, of course, is that they've made things difficult for our rivals, even if we must eventually face them if we want to dominate the region."

Another image appeared, this time, of one of the Akiaten. There was nothing unusual in the rendering as far as Hayden could tell, nothing to connect it to the strange, agile movements of the figures in the video, but there was something unnerving about the face on the screen all the same. Perhaps it was the bandana covering the mouth and nose, reaching down past the jaw, the lack of features making the eyes seem more intense than they would have otherwise.

He gauged the reactions of the others in the room. Nibiru was simply considering, her face thoughtful, her fingers drumming absently against the tabletop. Laine and Mitchell were wearing almost matching looks of calm anticipation, though Hayden imagined their reasons were very different. He knew that both had surety in their skills, but in the case of Laine at least, he could tell she was cautiously pleased at the thought of a challenging job. Not just offing freelancers who dove in over their heads.

He felt his own interest stirring as well.

Offense instead of defense would be a nice change. Yet another personality quirk among the elite slingers, that they couldn't just rest on their laurels. Hayden imagined he had more in common with the alpha augments than he'd care to admit.

"We have confirmed that there are several groups of these Akiaten and that they have cells in both the jungle and the city. You should also be aware that they have their fair share of contacts and supporters among the local citizens."

Bascilica motioned with one hand, and the display winked seamlessly back to the logo they had begun with.

"As I said, we don't know much about them, but we've marked their known hotspots in the files we'll be sending you. You'll all be updated on any further information we receive." He smiled. "Or outlandish stories we confirm."

Captain Mitchell grunted a small sound of dissent at that, the look on his face close to mutinous. He clearly didn't like the thought of the organization taking such obvious bullshit even semi-seriously. Hayden was simply intrigued.

Bascilica had asked for questions, but he was already checking his watch, and Hayden knew that any answers they received would be rushed and just as scripted as the bulk of his speech. Most likely, requests for elaboration would be met with more assurances that they would be updated with any necessary information. The executive gave them all a trademarked, stamped on smile, before picking up his bag and leaving the room with a sweeping wave.

The silence only lasted several heartbeats.

"Didn't get much about the source of the energy source from him, did we?" Captain Mitchell said.

"They forgot to feed him that line," Hayden offered, and the man smirked, as slight and thin as one of Laine's quick smiles, as though he worried the wrong person might see.

Nibiru's eyes came back to the room, slotting into focus on her surroundings as she closed her heads-up display. "It means 'Climbers.'"

Mitchell pinned her with a look. "What?"

"Akiaten," she answered, unconcerned as she slotted her rig into her small pack and slung it over her shoulder. "The closest translation. It's a Tagalog word, the indigenous language."

Hayden watched as Laine filed the newest bit of information away. "Wonder why that wasn't in the briefing?" he questioned. "Unless the guys in charge don't know how to run a translation." He wouldn't have been surprised, honestly.

"They probably don't want us spreading any ghost stories," Nibiru suggested, "Abilities, as Bascilica put it. I'm not usually a field operative, but they'll want to keep our curiosity to a minimum, right?"

Laine looked thoughtful but stayed quiet. It was unlike her to linger for more than a moment after a briefing and Hayden was surprised she had stayed behind this long.

It was Captain Mitchell who spoke next. "I'm not sure what he was playing at. But it doesn't seem like showing us that clip would help much with avoiding pre-conceived notions about their combat capabilities, or our inherent curiosity," His tone was exasperated. The man had little patience, especially when it came to what he perceived as the incompetence of others. "As long as bullets still work," he said, "I'll hold up my end."

Mitchell stood after he had finished speaking, pushing his chair back from the table with a screech and walking to the door. "I'll catch you all over there. Don't fuck around too long, or you'll miss your flight."

As if they would go without us, Hayden thought, looking from Laine to Nibiru. He had done a score of jobs with Laine and trusted her work implicitly. But he had a good feeling about the engineer. Her calm competence would be an asset to the team in a rough spot, and he was curious to see what she could do with CodeSource in the field.

Nibiru was standing as well, slinging a bag she had carried with her over one arm. "He's probably right about the leaving. When I see you guys again, we'll commence with kicking ass." She left the door ajar as she left.

"I'll send you her file if you're curious," Laine said to Hayden without looking at him, "But I've read it. She's good."

He nodded in acknowledgment, pushed his chair back, but didn't stand. "You look excited." That wasn't the right word, not quite. Laine looked more like a predator about to embark on a hunt.

"It's not often there's an unknown element to contend with. It's...," she trailed off.

"A challenge," he finished. "What do you think? About the side-stepping, he did about the 'climbers'. I mean, obviously they don't have superpowers, but the vid didn't look doctored."

Hayden started to continue, but Laine cut him off with a small noise of consideration. "Whatever it is, it might not be traditionally explainable, but it would be stupid of us to disregard the threat. If they, these Akiaten, believe it, then I say it's real enough."

3

The area, neighborhood, or district, whatever you wanted to call it, that HQ stood in, was a shithole, there was nothing else to call it, no other words to substitute.

Against the backdrop of cracked windows, crumbling sidewalks, and street signs peppered with bullet holes, even the shiny, clean, black of the car that dropped him off looked too bright to be real, like a splash of color in an old film.

The streets of his home in New Los Angeles were swept clean every day by a legion of maintenance drones, were empty of the garbage and the skinny, wandering dogs he glimpsed here. He'd only seen real poverty in vids and the sight of it unnerved him.

The HQ was mostly underground, but that was hardly a surprise. Hayden had stopped being shocked at the places the Union Americana team staked out years ago, but he had never been more impressed than he was with this setup.

For as raw as the construction the site looked on the outside, the hustle and bustle of workers and materials provided the perfect cover. The fact that it was a busy construction project, seemingly run and staffed by a local firm and yet completely under the control of the Union, was evidence of the vast amounts of resources being poured into this mission.

He wasn't sure if they'd commissioned the place themselves for appearance's sake, or simply bought out an actual project, sent the real workers and owners off to parts unknown. Or perhaps they simply paid them off, like they had the rest of the country. Union Americana maintained so many subsidiaries that it was all but impossible to tell. Considering how complicated the webs of commerce were in this post-war world it was possible that the Union had bought the property from E-Bloc or Asia Prime without anyone realizing it. Such was the layer cake that was modern corporate rule.

en they try some high-end stealth insertion. Better to take it slow and build this op from the ground up instead of coming in hot E-Bloc style, especially since E-Bloc beat them to that particular punch.

Still, he would have gladly taken a quicker flight rather than the extravagant room. While the luxuries were nice, he would have happily slept anywhere with a mattress and a shower. As much work as this mission was bound to be, he'd likely spend most of his time in whatever room they had set aside for him to work. On earlier jobs, he'd often fall asleep after a hack with the jack still in and CodeSource still running. It was close to dark and though he felt the fuzzy fog of jetlag, he wasn't in the mood to sleep. He'd dozed off on the plane several times, missing the view of the ocean beneath them despite his window seat.

Hayden unpacked a few of his things, shoving them into the top drawer of the rich, brown dresser, but left most of it in his bag, along with the supplies he would need for his job. No doubt Union Americana would provide him with anything he asked for, but he trusted the equipment he had bought himself and liked having no obligation to return it.

Hayden slipped the bag over one shoulder, plucked the keycard he'd been issued from where he'd tossed it on the bedside table, and headed out the door.

Nibiru sat in the hallway, a few doors down, her back against one wall, the black soles of her boots scuffing on the carpet as she shifted at the sound of his door shutting and latching. She closed the laptop that sat on her legs and looked up.

"Wasn't sure which room was yours," she said, by way of explanation. "It's too much, right? All I need to do my job is a computer and some cash, and here I am with a hot tub."

He raised one eyebrow. "They gave you a hot tub?"

She grinned, quick and then gone. "No, but they might as well have. You?"

Hayden shook his head. "Laine probably has one. They wouldn't try it with Mitchell though. He'd consider it an insult."

She huffed a laugh and stood, tucking her computer into the brown messenger bag that hung at her side, touching the jack in the back of her neck absently, though there was not a cable there. He often found himself doing the same when he thought of work, or whenever he had the urge to immerse him in the addictive world of MassNet.

"I haven't looked around yet, other than the walk up here. Like I said, they usually keep me in a workshop or a pilot box, this clandestine operative thing is new for me. Mind if I join you?"

"Sure," he answered, "I'm just gonna head further down." He flashed the card he'd been given and nodded at hers where it stuck slightly out of her pocket. "Let's see what these open."

In the end, it wasn't much. Hayden wasn't sure why he expected anything different than the usual set up. Everyone had their own job to do, and likely it was Mitchell's security protocols that limited access by department.

Their work-spaces were nice enough, private rooms that were empty except for several types of seating, a desk, and a hologram port that could be used to project his work into something larger or to view incoming calls or messages without having to leave the room.

Nibiru's was across from his, and she explored it with the door open, making a joke about having a mini fridge while he did not. (There was no mini fridge in either room).

Further exploration of the building led them to many locked doors. Some seemed unguarded and opened into a dark, puddled alleyways. Finally, they came to a large room with dozens of servers and several focused looking individuals milling about setting them up. They stopped working at Hayden and Nibiru's entrance. A few of them were people Hayden recognized, though they weren't part of his team. Nibiru gave an awkward wave and backed out, Hayden following.

"Guess we're early," she said. "I didn't expect there to be this much sitting around. Was kind of hoping, we'd hop off the plane and get straight to it."

Hayden shrugged with only one shoulder. "Union Americana is all about appearances. They'll have to make it look good first."

Her only response was a sigh, as she leaned against the wall, her bag swaying slightly as she adjusted the strap.

"I haven't seen Laine yet," he offered. "Knowing her, she's already broken protocol and is out there in the city doing recon on the locals. I bet they flew her in on the jet."

That at least seemed to appease Nibiru. She gave a considering nod and stood up straighter. "Well," she said, "It'll take me at least an hour to find my way back to my room. By the time I do that and read over those new files they sent, maybe they'll need us. You coming?"

He shook his head. "Nah. I'm actually starving. I know there's food here, but I think I'll check out the local fare. I saw some vendors a few blocks over when they were bringing us in."

She raised both eyebrows, her voice teasing. "Sneaking out, huh? You'll be lucky if they send a jet for you ever again." She began walking away but called over her shoulder. "Bring me something back, if it's any good."

The place was so quiet that her footsteps seemed to echo, even on the carpet.

Hayden's sense of direction was better than the engineer's, and it took him no time at all to retrace his steps to the back-alley doors they had discovered earlier.

He moved quietly, the silence of the building making each step and breath seem gunshot loud. He was glad of his caution when he found two members of the security team, whom he was not supposed to wander around without, talking together in the threshold.

The next door he tried was unguarded and he slipped out easily enough, double-checking that he still had his ID in case someone unfamiliar tried to stop him at the door upon re-entry. He had been with the company long enough that he recognized many of the soldiers and security teams, and they recognized him in turn, but on the off chance that someone new halted him, his characteristic breach of protocol would be extremely frowned upon.

Hayden and Laine were both known for being rule breakers, and while Bascilica seemed to prize them for that quality, they had never run an op with Mitchell. Somehow, Hayden doubted Captain Mitchell would be so accommodating.

He walked the first few blocks through the alleyways, weaving around an overturned dumpster and narrowly avoiding a collision with a yellow cat that seemed more than a little blind. He pressed himself to the wall as a child surged past, chasing after it and calling out a word that Hayden didn't understand.

The street he finally stepped into was a little wider than the one he'd started out on; there was room for a bit of sun to make its way down between the rooftops.

He felt almost uncomfortably warm once he stepped out of the shadowed area. He began walking toward a stall where something smelled intriguingly like fried meat of some sort. As he walked closer, he could tell that it was pork, which was good enough reason to stick around as far as Hayden was concerned. He might be a high-end slinger and wealthy by most any standard of the world, but synthetic food was common fare, and anytime he got a chance to eat real food out in the world he would.

Normally, the Union kept him within its own borders, so it was pre-packaged and highly processed foodstuffs like every other 'advanced' part of post-war civilization. However, Hayden had found that it was always the shitholes that progress had skipped over that had the best food. It might be cheap, it might have some questionable ingredients, but it was honest, and he liked that. It was worth a slap on the wrist from the Captain if it came to that.

He positioned himself at the back of the line, behind an older man with a rumpled shirt and hair that was going gray at the temples, and waited for his turn. The man turned back once but simply looked at him curiously before returning his attention to the cart.

Hayden had his hoodie over his head, so none of the folks in line could see his ports, as a place like this probably didn't have much in the way of advanced tech and it wouldn't do to get made on day one of the ops.

While he waited, he let his eyes take in the area, wincing when he spotted a distant block of houses where shipping containers seemed to be the dominant construction material.

The line moved forward, and he kept his eyes on the cart, his hunger and his impatience growing as the smell grew stronger. When his turn to order came, he simply said, "Three," and held up the correct number of fingers, figuring that two for himself and one for Nibiru would be plenty. On the off chance that Laine had appeared before he returned and was in the mood for food or company, he might be willing to relinquish one of his own.

He knew that Laine would never stoop to 'sneaking out for a bite' like he had. He wasn't about to point out to her that 'sneaking out for some recon' was just her spin on the same infraction. She would eat the food provided by Hayden gladly enough before breaking protocol to try the local cuisine.

Hayden watched the man cook the pork up, before rolling it together with peppers and vegetables, and then frying the dough it lay inside to hold the creation together. Standing there, he was almost hungry enough to order a fourth, but he figured the family in line behind him wouldn't appreciate the added wait. The cook finished up and passed him a brown paper bag, so heavy that he half worried the combination of the grease and the weight would make the bottom give way before he made it back.

He was in the process of walking further down the street, toward someone selling something unidentifiable on a stick, when he caught sight of a group of E-Bloc soldiers speaking with two of the locals, their voices too far away for him to make out words but the threat of violence was in their tone.

He was in the process of walking further down the street, toward someone selling something unidentifiable on a stick, when he heard the sound of a gun being fired.

There was no other sound in the world like it. Unmistakable. Powerful.

Far down the street, a group of E-Bloc soldiers was speaking with two of the locals, their voices too far away for him to make out more than the threat of violence in their tone.

He ducked his head, tightening the hood of his jacket. As he walked across the street he remained mostly facing the group of people waiting for the vendor to give them their attention, but his ears were on the soldiers.

The vendor was as distracted as Hayden, having forestalled exchanging food for money as he watched the commotion escalate.

The E-Bloc soldiers were too close to HQ for comfort. The questions they asked were likely about other outsiders, unfamiliar cars. As he watched, he saw the soldier in charge cycle through a series of images on a screen he held up to the man he was questioning, asking questions to accompany each one.

As the first man started to nervously answer, the sound of gunfire came from one block over, the opposite direction from where Union Americana lay.

Hayden had been in enough dangerous places during his years with Americana that the sound had become familiar. And what did that say about his line of work? The rapid pop, pop, pop, that grew louder as it grew closer. The sound of screams as civilians grabbed their friends by the hands or their children by the wrists and hauled them off the streets, into open storefronts and alleys, or behind cars and stalls.

Hayden found his own cover in the nearest break between two buildings, not even wide enough to be called an alley. A local woman was already hiding there but stepped back when she saw him coming.

When he glanced back, she was slipping into a side door, gesturing for him to follow. He nodded in thanks but waved the concern away. The gunfire was moving closer, and he wanted to see who the fight was between. There was no way he'd make it back into HQ without getting stopped by security, so he was already humped as far as getting busted for sneaking out was concerned, so he might as well come to the chopping block with some useful intel.

If Union Americana was involved he would have already been receiving a message either warning him of the danger or requesting his help.

The woman shook her head, door slamming shut, as Hayden turned to watch, his back pressed tight to the rough, crumbling brick of the building.

The gunfire moved closer, close enough to hurt his ears. Used to the sound or not, he found himself wincing at each loud spray of shots. Laine was the only person he knew who never flinched at the noise, not even the slightest tightening of her eyes. He was a slinger, so his experience with violence tended to be somewhat removed. The few times he'd been in the thick of things, he'd always had Laine by his side, protecting him.

He saw the E-Bloc troopers first, clothing camouflaged to blend in with the green of the jungle contrasting greatly with the varied shades of gray that made up the sidewalks and streets, the faded paint that covered the stalls and storefronts.

Many of the soldiers jogged backward, firing rounds and lobbing grenades as they went. Those closest to the perceived threat ran without trying to aim, firing occasional shots over their shoulders. They were spooked beyond belief, and that was saying something considering the grueling training the E-Bloc troopers endured. For them to break with combat discipline was a big deal, and it made him deeply concerned with what might be snapping at their heels.

He watched a man trip and then scramble to his feet, boots pounding the asphalt, barely grasping his weapon again before he ran.

The gap between the running soldiers and the threat behind them lasted scarcely five seconds.

From their covered faces to their fluid movements, there was no mistaking what they were.

Akiaten.

He'd kept a copy of the footage that Bascilica had shown them during the briefing, and in his wait before the flight had watched it several times, hoping to glean something new on each run through.

There had been more sent to them as promised, typed up neatly in a compressed file, but the information had been more about the location than the locals, and there had been next to nothing about the Akiaten that Bascilica himself had not told them already. A few updates regarding theories on where their headquarters might be located, but nothing that helped him now.

In the space between the buildings, he felt safe enough. He was unarmed and dressed enough like a civilian that there was nothing to attract their attention. Should they approach him for some reason, the only indication that he belonged to Union Americana was the ID card he carried.

Manila was a diverse enough place, had been pre-war and certainly was post-war, as many who could not fully adjust to life in the corporate societies of the world fled into a diaspora that spanned the globe. At the thought, he pushed the ID deeper into his pocket and watched the Akiaten approach, heralded by increasingly sporadic gunfire.

One of them, he noted, carried nothing but knives. The band of Akiaten crashed into the E-Bloc squad, coming at them from a multitude of angles, as some ran vertically on the walls of nearby buildings even as others vaulted cars and shop stalls while firing wildly.

Their weapons weren't the cutting-edge firearms of the corporate world, instead, the Akiaten seemed to be carrying mostly civilian grade firearms.

Places like the Philippines had not been disarmed the way many 'civilized' regions of the world had, and it looks like these climbers had stockpiled.

Mostly he saw revolvers, semi-automatic pistols, and shotguns, which should have been child's play when going up against the high-end tools carried by the E-Bloc troopers. However, the Akiaten were dishing out damage with hideous effectiveness, and Hayden realized that these local resistance fighters had been wildly underestimated.

Four members of the E-Bloc squad were already on the ground, two of them bleeding, one of them still. Hayden's eyes locked onto an Akiaten with a red bandana tied around his nose and mouth, tracking his progress down the road. It was easier to focus on one, rather than the group of ten or so that barreled down the street.

Red's eyes trained onto an E-Bloc soldier who had slowed his running to frantically reload his gun. The soldier had just slotted the clip into place when the Akiaten leaped, grabbed onto the horizontal bar of an old streetlight, and swung his legs forward. One foot crunched into the soldier's throat, the other found his chest and slammed the soldier back. The man with the red bandana let go at the height of his arc, landed on top of the soldier to drive a knife into the man's throat, then seamlessly kept running, already locked onto his next target.

The remaining E-Bloc soldiers had rallied together, using two cars parked bumper to bumper for cover as they fired what bullets remained to them.

The Akiaten slowed their advance as one of their number was riddled with bloody holes and fell to the pavement. The resistance fighters stuck back to the shadows that were rising as the sun neared the horizon's edge. They fired the few guns they had themselves, threw broken bottles, and a smoke grenade. The occasional member still surged forward to fight with gun and blade, leaving two more soldiers and another fighter dead on the ground, but the brief flash of battle was winding down as it became clear that the E-Bloc soldiers were dug in.

While the Akiaten assault may have been furious, its power had broken once the more heavily armed and armored E-Bloc soldiers were able to catch their breath and set up a legitimate fire defense.

The last Akiaten faded into the shadows, dragging away the bodies of their dead just as a military grade vehicle arrived to pull the E-Bloc soldiers out.

Hayden took his chance and stepped back into the street, shoulders tensing unconsciously as he thought of another rain of bullets. None came, and he was able to get a glimpse of two of the Akiaten retreating together, their movements still unnervingly fluid, the way Laine moved sometimes, but it seemed more unconscious than her careful, constant precision. As they turned onto a small side street, he watched as one ran for several steps upon the side of the building, his body nearly sideways.

The street grew quiet as the E-Bloc soldiers pulled out. The locals who had rushed to the sidelines began to trickle back out, speaking with each other in small groups, voices hushed and edged with more excitement, he thought, than fear. There was pride in some of their tones, even though much of the street and the shops had been shot up or otherwise damaged in the violent exchange, and he made a note of that.

Hayden adjusted his grip on the bag of food, rolling the top over several times to trap the escaping heat, and began the walk back to HQ.

A sense of anticipation settled over him. If that was what the Akiaten could do on the streets, he was ready to see what they could do with code. He shook his head and walked faster, smiling slightly.

He was beginning to sound like Laine.

At the door, security raised their eyebrows. He held up the bag of food in answer. Hayden was prepared to dig his ID out for verification, but the man who waved him through looked familiar, Reice, he thought maybe, and the man recognized his him in return.

"Sounds like it got pretty hot out there," Reice said. "You okay, Cole? Cap would have your ass if it was anybody but me on this door."

"I'm in one piece at least, and thanks for that brother," Hayden answered. "It was a bunch of E-Bloc troopers, sniffing around. Got ambushed by the locals we were briefed about. I'm sure they'll send us an update before morning."

When he knocked on Nibiru's door, he had the story ready, the words already arranged. But she simply accepted the food with a smile and a nod and retreated into her room, where he could see the glow of several screens bathing the chamber in unearthly light. Already at work this one. Well so much for bringing food and being charming, he thought with a rueful grin.

Ears still ringing with gunfire, Hayden returned to his own room and ate his share while plugging his jack into the system and pulling up the files that Bascilica had sent.

There was still no information, he was sure, but it wouldn't hurt to look deeper.

4

The next day was comprised of a series of meetings briefing everyone on the mission for Union Americana in Manila, with all its new updates, rules, and bells and whistles tacked on.

Bascilica was risking everything on this op, his reputation, his job, and even big parts of his own personal fortune. He wanted it made clear that this was a game played for keeps.

Life in the safe house now came with a score of restrictions on all interactions with the locals, including, but not limited to, armed escorts for key operatives and only mission specific outings would be authorized.

Most of it was standard procedure with clandestine deployments like this, but Hayden felt like a little kid caught with his hand in the cookie jar.

The movements of the E-Block soldiers were also addressed. Their patrols had increased in frequency in the last twenty-four hours, in addition to a general hardening of their known safe houses and deployment centers.

Soon Hayden found himself summoned to a small room deep in the bowels of the HQ, only moments after being briefed on its existence, which told him two things, they knew less about the attack than they said, and through him, were hoping to learn more about the Akiaten; the second, was that Reice, the guard at the door when Hayden returned, was not to be trusted with any more sensitive information.

It would likely be hard for Hayden to leave the building without a tail unless he was on official business, and even then, it seemed like the Captain intended to shackle them with details.

Hayden was relieved when Captain Mitchell walked in after Hayden had been escorted into the room. Mitchell was as by-the-book as they came, but he was easy to talk to. Hayden preferred being debriefed by him rather than some security asshole with an inflated sense of his own importance and a stick up his ass. (Maybe he was still bitter about the snitching. He should have snagged some extra food to buy the Reice's silence).

The room was comfy enough, plain white walls, two chairs on opposite ends of a table, and a couch tucked into the corner. Mitchell sat and folded his hands, one over the other.

"So, I don't merit a room with a two way, mirror?" Hayden asked, an edge of a smirk in his voice, though he didn't permit his lips to show it.

Mitchell did not look close to laughing, but neither was his answer hostile. "It's just a de-briefing, Cole. They want a statement about everything you saw yesterday, during the attack.

And before you ask, nobody, tipped us off. So, consider yourself a man with friends on the security team, even if we can narrow it down to just a few suspects. I don't expect you to divulge that name either, it's irrelevant to the matter at hand. We were reviewing the footage the traffic cams caught. Nibiru is indeed quite the whiz with physical systems, and she's a team player. You're not as discreet as you think slinger."

"I didn't exactly have the presence of mind to record it, Mitchell. The details are gonna be dicey, and I wasn't in a position to see it that well."

Captain Mitchell shrugged, his expression unperturbed. "You don't want to deal with this de-briefing bullshit, be more careful next time you slip out to buy a banana-on-a-stick or whatever local fare you've convinced yourself isn't crawling with parasites and carcinogens. You think I wouldn't rather be doing something else?" When his only answer was a slight sigh from the slinger, Mitchell moved on. "Besides, even if you didn't think something was useful, it might be to us. Or it might come in handy later. E-Bloc we're familiar with, plenty of engagements and intel in the Union database to paint a precise picture, but we still know next to nothing about these Akiaten. To date, you are the only Union member in good standing to experience a first-hand encounter with them."

"Can't you have your team player, Nibiru, bring up more of the street cams?" asked Hayden with a slightly exasperated tone, as he was not accustomed to being talked to this way by anybody. Well maybe Overdog, but that bastard was a slinger of the old school and could say pretty much whatever he wanted to pretty much whoever he wanted. "I probably have work I should be doing, right?"

"An unknown slinger or slingers came through the wires and hit the street cam central storage database. High-level government hack. Nibiru says that unless they were standing next to her and hardwired into the cams the assault had to come through MassNet," snapped Captain Mitchell, his patience already wearing thin, "Which means there are heavy duty slingers on the board now. I'd say that yes, you probably do have work you should be doing right now, but be that as it may, your eyewitness account is all we have. So, spill it, Cole."

There wasn't much of an argument for that. Hayden sat back, and let Mitchell record the words as he said them, listing the sight and sounds outside the HQ, the people he'd seen in the crowd. An entire day had passed but could recall some of it fairly vividly. The man in front of him in line, the family behind him, and the woman who tried to usher him through the side-door in the alleyway. He remembered the color of a shirt here, a child ducking into their father's side there. The number of E-Bloc soldiers and the Akiaten were, he thought, mostly accurate. He remembered the general but not the specific. He could tell Mitchell what the soldiers had done but not the name of the maneuvers.

As a slinger, he'd never learned the difference between a screen or attack by fire, or a movement to contact or objective assault. As for the Akiaten, he had learned nothing new about them and had nothing to add aside from comments (careful not to sound too impressed) for their skill and enthusiasm.

Nothing they could do that an alpha augment couldn't duplicate, though he decided not to point out that the amount of investment capital that would have been required to augment that many alphas would have been astronomical. Laine was a solo, and she had cost a fortune.

Considering that cost though, he suddenly began to suspect the warriors he'd seen locked in battle against the E-Bloc troopers were probably not cyborgs at all. He knew the direction they had retreated in, but that was hardly worth noting, being urban insurgents there was no doubt that they'd spread out, double back, and do their best to disappear into the sprawl.

Despite the recording in progress, Mitchell took notes on a pad in scrawl so sloppy that Hayden could scarcely recognize it as the English language. Hayden had no idea what the older man planned to do it except to haul it around for his own benefit. There weren't paper files anymore, and it was the recording that the executives and the security heads would end up listening to, or adding to the database should there be anything remotely useful in his rambling. Hayden doubted it. No sir, these words were just for the captain himself, and something about that made Hayden nervous.

Finishing up his scribbling, Mitchell cut the recording off in the lingering silence, slid his pen through the thin metal spiral that held the pages of his notepad together. He placed the book into an interior pocket of his jacket, before snatching the recording as well and giving Hayden the same unimpressed look he had begun with.

"Let's not do this again," he said.

"No promises."

The Captain's face hardened. "I'm serious, Cole."

Hayden wasn't surprised to see Nibiru on his way back to the room that housed his workspace. She looked to be on her way back from another part of the building, a large box, its contents indiscernible, balanced in her arms. Just starting out, they would have had her working on something important, he was curious as to the details.

"Hey," she greeted. "Did they dig out the polygraph?"

"Not this time. I just had to relay the exciting tale again. I think they're taking me at my word finally."

"That's probably a mistake on their part," she said, keying open the door.

"Just be glad I didn't list you as an accomplice. I could have been out of that line and back at HQ if you hadn't wanted me to bring you something."

She huffed, kicked open the door, and walked inside to set the bag down.

"You need any help?" he offered, just for something to say. He was itching for a continuum of yesterday's excitement and would have liked to see what job their higher-ups had set her on. It had to be more interesting than tracking down a co-worker's rule-breaking, then again, finding out a bunch of hard systems got fried through MassNet had to be pretty adrenaline rush inducing. He was certainly piqued.

Nibiru's face was incredulous, though she seemed to think he was teasing. "I'm your backup, remember. Sorry the powers that be had me dime you out with the cam footage, nothing I could do about that. Besides, you'd be hopeless at my job, unless there's something you're not telling me. Go code something," she said. She left the door open but turned her back to dig the bag.

Shaking his head, smiling a bit, Hayden returned to his own workspace and fitted the cables to his jacks. Today had not gone in Hayden's favor so far, but maybe a few hours getting his CodeSource fortress built and looking pretty would turn things around.

Hayden woke at 4 in the morning to the sound of an alarm he hadn't set. The sound was tinny and insistent and he shut it off without looking, before dragging himself upright. He already knew it was some sort of security breech; bad enough to be deemed an emergency if they were waking them up instead of meeting at 8 or so the next day, as was usual. Then he looked anyway, just to confirm there was no mistake. The words 'E-Block hacking attempt' were enough to rouse him further.

He swung his legs to one side and stood, flipping the switch to light the room and stepping into the first pair of pants he dug out of his drawer. His shirt tugged over his head, he stepped into the bathroom long enough to assure that it wasn't inside out and reentered the living space to grab his bag from the couch.

No time to perform the usual morning routines, which he was not pleased about, but it's not like a slinger really had to be presentable to get the job done anyway.

A clamor sounded at the end of the hallway. Nibiru stumbled out her room, pulling it closed with a bang, then pausing to stare at the door as if affronted by the unnecessary noise. Her clothes looked slept in, and her hair was wild, bits of blue sticking up haphazardly on the side that wasn't buzzed to almost nothing. She caught him looking, blinked tiredly at him, and tugged a hat over the mess of hair.

"They called you, too?" he asked.

"I'm your back-up, remember? You have to wake up at 4 in the morning, so do I. Guess I'm supposed to take over if you fall asleep at the keyboard."

She walked beside him, feet dragging, one shoulder brushing the smooth, newly painted wall as she went.

"If it helps," he offered, "There's usually coffee, and not that organic Columbian garbage, but real deal Union synthetic hydro."

Her face brightened considerably.

When they reached the downstairs room, they had scoped out the previous day, Hayden was not surprised to see Nibiru disregard their supervisor where he stood waiting and make a beeline for the pot sitting on a table to one side.

To say that the atmosphere in the room was chaotic would be an understatement. Members of the security teams and other people rushed back and forth, not running, but walking with quick, hurried steps that were just as obvious in their haste.

Hayden made his way to Overdog where the man stood overseeing a group of slingers, all of them jacked into CodeSource. Overdog was taller even than Hayden, but so scrawny in other areas that he always looked as though he'd been sick for a long while. What Overdog lacked in physical prowess, he made up for in his intimidating manner when displeased, he could make his voice sharp enough to draw blood. The man's arms were crossed and his jaw was tight.

Internally, Hayden winced at the sight of him. It normally took a lot to rattle the man and he knew that if it were a routine problem, the group sitting with the supervisor would have been able to handle it without him. As it was, it looked as though they were barely holding it together in his absence. Even if he were not as skilled as he was, another person working the problem would help. Sometimes, if you spent too long in the code, everything started to look the same and you became immune to seeing the answer. Sometimes, a fresh pair of eyes was all it took to solve the riddle.

"Fill me in," he said, letting his feet stop him in front of Overdog. One of the slingers looked up at him, eyes focused and shoulders relaxing before she turned her attention back to her heads-up display.

"The attack started twenty-five minutes ago. It took ten minutes for the slackers on duty here to even get wise," Overdog barked at the handful of slingers frantically immersed in their CodeSource trance, "To isolate the threat and determine that backup was necessary. You were called as soon as they confirmed the severity of the issue."

Hayden looked around at the slingers in question—three men and two women, some at desks, some sprawled on a couch by the door, and a third sitting on the floor with his back against the wall, fingers moving fast and loud as machine gun fire in the quiet room. There had been chatter when he entered, as they rose from the code to speak to their supervisor or one another before returning their full attention to the system, but now that Overdog was explaining the urgency of the situation, they had taken it upon themselves to keep silent, lest they waste time repeating an explanation.

"We're certain at this point that the attack was launched by E-Bloc. Our people have been working to build up our hard network, drawing down from the local grid but in such a way that nobody would notice. The usual insertion job, but honestly, we've had to sink a few of our own nodes in the area. It's like this place never caught up with the rest of the world, so there isn't a ton of infrastructure to piggy-back off. Everything is set now, so you'll be able to get to work finding this energy source, but only if we can keep the hard network intact. E-Bloc has sliced through the low-level firewalls and is trying to seize control of all the systems confined to this neighborhood, from basic government infrastructure and on into the handful of private citizen nodes. Likely in response to the attack last night."

"E-Bloc has no style," Hayden snorted. "It's like every one of their people went to the scorched earth school of computer science. What have they hit so far?" Hayden asked Overdog, staring intently at the slinger closest to him, the woman who had looked up briefly at his arrival. She was deep in the code now, and past hearing the conversation. She appeared to be solid, and from what he could see in the wild scroll of her screen certainly worthy of having a place on a clandestine op, even if she and the others didn't catch the incoming hack and slash until it was nearly ten minutes underway.

"One of them said something I didn't catch, D- something. You'll see when you get in there. Which you should do." There was a hint of stress in Overdog's voice, a rarely witnessed anomaly. Even rarer was the fact that he did not bother to hide it. D-something likely meant denial of service, though Hayden wasn't sure what they hoped to accomplish with that, other than locking them out of the system, as they'd just sync back in later when the heat was off. Denial of service attacks best aimed at large corporations, who would lose money being offline, to attack the small Union Americana Mainframe itself would be effective, but this HQ was just a small cell of hackers, soldiers, and general staffers with their own server that existed independently of the central Mainframe. It was, however, an easy way to overwhelm the small number of slingers on call for the night.

Hayden heard paper rustling behind him and turned to his left to find Nibiru settling down at an empty table, ripping the wrapper off a muffin as she clunked her mug of coffee down. She took a quick, large bite, and chewed while she unpacked her rig.

"You gonna let me beat you in there?" she asked, and her eyes already looked brighter.

He sat his own bag on the opposite end of the table and pulled his computer free, opening it and logging in in the space of five seconds. She grinned at him encouragingly. "You handle it then, boss. I'll kick some stuff your way if I can help." This was not MassNet, but he understood her meaning and appreciated the offer.

He pulled his cable from the bag, attached one end to the computer and the other to the jack in his neck. There was a slight jolt as the connection took, not unpleasant, not quite what he would call a shock, a sort of hum just under his skin, a subsonic vibration in his skull that he knew would last the duration of the hack. The sensation used to rattle him, but he had grown used to it and craved it when he went without it. The first kiss of cyber space, he thought to himself and smiled as he felt the edges of the trance begin to take hold.

Hayden opened the program he needed, bypassing the one tacked on by Union Americana when he joined the company. Going instead, for the one he had used for the last ten years. He periodically added his own modifications to the programming, updating as the slingers he had to contend with grew more advanced.

It wasn't protocol. It was such a signature of his that if Overdog ever caught Hayden slicing with anything else, the supervisor would probably have him hollowed out on the spot as a traitor.

The code rose up like the sea, waves washing over his head, and in seconds he was immersed in familiar waters. He felt the part of his mind not focused on slinging divorce itself from the proceedings, paying a minuscule amount of attention to his surroundings, so that, should something go wrong in real time, he could come out of his daze and deal with it accordingly.

It would take a lot to rouse him though, save for the completion of his goal. The jack was the best Union Americana could afford, which was saying something, and it had been custom made to his individual brain wave patterns. One for CodeSource and one, the most expensive, for MassNet.

The ultra-high-end jacks allowed him to channel nearly all his focus into the job at hand. Crafted as they were, specifically to him, it allowed him to code faster than many less well-funded slingers could dream of.

The sum of the two together pretty much meant that if Hayden ever decided to break his non-compete and non-disclosure contracts he'd be a dead man.

The symbols scrolled past and he took the dive forward, drowning himself in the task. He blew through the walls of code, fingers flying with him, driving his progress forward.

Having once taken his board through and out of the fledgling Union system, he moved his focus of control through the municipal hard systems. He took a wide path, first slipping through the street cams, whose security had already been torn full of holes by whoever had fried the databases that rested in whatever government vault housed the feeds.

Nobody was watching the cams, near as he could tell, no errant lines of code or non-essential algorithms were present in the rapid scroll before him.

From there Hayden accessed a private wireless signal that allowed him to bounce around the handful of others in the neighborhood until he was able to crawl his way into the back door of a basic services grid. The system was so old it was almost primitive, considering what was available in Union Americana, even to its poorest citizens.

He was able to find rudimentary weather controls for the government habitats where most people lived, though he found that much of the power and individual housing unit controls had been either sliced via the hardware or degraded entirely.

Hayden found himself trying to recall a quote by Gibson, one of the greats of many generations ago, something about how the future was already here but was unevenly distributed. Something like that, and it certainly seemed to hold true here. That meant that nobody was going to expect him to erupt out of such a degraded system.

He had to move carefully, make his movements, his changes, in the system hard to track. It would be simpler if he could meet his objective without the E-Block hackers realizing their plans were being foiled. If they caught onto his presence and his motives, they might just shut down the whole thing rather than risk their own security. It was all dependent upon how deeply in the system they were entrenched.

He wasn't sure what, exactly, they were looking for, but after a few moments of observation no assaults were launched on the hard systems that they had now forced access to. If they'd been on the hunt for a clandestine Union operation they'd be coming at this through MassNet, slipping through the wires and into their software network, spoiling for a fight.

As it was, they stayed exclusively in CodeSource, approaching their supposed opponent through the hard systems in the neighborhood. They were definitely looking for someone though, Hayden realized, as he watched the E-Bloc slingers bring down the entire grid one habitat at a time.

Out there, in the world of flesh and blood, there were habitats full of people that suddenly lost power. Weather controls went out, doors locked, water stopped flowing, and everything blacked out. Likely each blackout in the system coincided with a physical search of the habitat, or at least some manner of recon, and that was not going to be good if it happened here.

He felt the inside of his cheek catch between his teeth, an unconscious, anticipatory tick. He had removed his jack several times before when the taste of blood startled him out of a hack. Hayden forced his jaw to relax.

Still brimming with excitement from the chase, he wove himself back into the columns of code. If E-Bloc wanted to play that game, then so could Hayden, and he had a room full of Union slingers at his back.

Once he spotted the alterations in the code, it was easy to track the E-Bloc hackers back to the window they'd slipped through. He took note of the problem, sent Overdog a memo detailing the slip in the defenses that they had found and exploited, and kept slicing. The other slingers caught on quickly to Hayden's plan, and as one section of the grid went dark Hayden and his own crew knocked out a second one, and then a third. If E-Bloc wanted to play fast and loose with hard systems, then so could the Union.

He couldn't help the stab of annoyance he felt at the other slingers hired on by Americana for even letting this blunt sort of assault get through the first firewall. He knew the mistake was an easy one, and he couldn't spend all his time in CodeSource. The extra hands were necessary and helpful. The problem and its difficulty were not their fault, but rather the fault of Union Americana as a whole.

He would be lucky, with so many E-Bloc hackers meshed in the system, to get out without a few mistakes of his own.

Nibiru was with him, her icon added to the slinger roster in his team roll up and Hayden brought her into the fold. The engineer took control of HQ's hard systems with the stroke of a few keys, her access slicing through the security walls built to keep non-essential staff from being able to run amok in the system. At Hayden's command, Nibiru activated the backup power, a closed-circuit system housed in HQ itself, just as the Union slingers blacked out the entire city block. Now that their area had been blacked, and without an open response, it was just another point on a map of other unremarkable sections of the city. Or at least that was Hayden's hope in the ruse.

E-Bloc seemed to have gotten the picture that another slinger force was in play, and they'd begun to slow their grid search. No doubt the troopers out there in the streets were circling up in anticipation of an attack, as their house-to-house plan had not only been discovered but aggressively and blatantly mimicked. Another block went down and Nibiru brought the HQ back onto grid power.

As the other slingers continued to black out and re-activate parts of the neighborhood at random, Hayden set to work on closing down the system to outside forces, kicking a few of the E-Bloc icons off the network with malicious strings of weaponized code. Unless the E-Bloc slingers were physically jacked into municipal systems his counter-attacks probably wouldn't kill any of the slingers, as CodeSource was somewhat limited to the physical systems and their onboard code. Still, a sudden zap to the jack, even though a surge protector, was enough to knock a slinger off the board for a day or two. The other Union slingers started to catch on, and as the E-Bloc slingers started to get pushed out of systems the net began to close, and they bolted.

Even with the jack still in, his focused expression slipped off and he felt himself smirk in satisfaction. They didn't get a thing. No intel on where the Union HQ was, or if it even existed. No line on the Akiaten either, which is what Hayden assumed they were trying to do, rooting out the insurgents a block at a time.

A relieved, rejoicing scatter of voices began to slip through his mental shield against distraction. A bit of the tension in his shoulders drained away as he reached back to pull his jack free.

Time spent in CodeSource was hard to regulate. He never felt it pass in the normal way. An hour could feel like minutes or a single hour might feel like days. It could be dangerous to lose track of it completely, could cause problems with the hardware that made up the jack. He had no doubt that if he lingered too long, the team still gathered in the room would have shaken him out of his stupor, but he needed to rest regardless, see the damage that had been done himself and explain the fix he'd just implemented to Overdog or anyone else who needed to know.

His fingers already beginning to tug on the cable, and he almost didn't notice the tag.

Almost.

5

Sun could have done her work one of the common cubicle farms that comprised the bulk of Asia Prime's primary Manila operations base, but being the organization's lead slinger came with certain perks, one of them being a private workspace with a plate glass window that could be shuttered while she did her work, or opened to enjoy the view of the city below her.

It wasn't much to look at during the day. The cityscape of Manila with its bland concrete and rudimentary pre-war architectural style failing by her estimation in comparison to the glittering grandeur of the Asia Prime mega-metros like Osaka or Beijing.

She could see the faintest edge of blue water in the distance and there was something to be said for the primitive beauty of this place. When the sun set it was at least a modest improvement in aesthetic. The haphazard lighting from the bustling city lit up the windows in various shades of gold and silver were pretty enough to waste time on. Prime had set aside space for her, and she wasn't about to let it go to waste.

There were at least a dozen other slingers currently working this hack, an attack on Union Americana's native servers, a mission to steal and destroy what intelligence they had on both E-Bloc and the local resistance cells, in addition to knocking their servers offline for as long as they could. If the opposition had to waste valuable time and resources on rebuilding their defenses, this only served the interests of Asia Prime, and if Sun managed to eliminate any opposition slingers in the process, there could very well be a bonus waiting for her at the end of the quarter.

They were close when Union Americana's stash of slingers began to come online, doing work that could only be described as damage control while they waited for someone higher up to make the real calls.

Deep in CodeSource herself, she had to trust that the slingers on her side were competent enough to hold their own without her input. The E-Bloc slinger cadre had initiated the hack, acting as the blunt instruments they were, waging a scorched earth campaign on the entire city sector in search of Akiaten safe houses, sympathizers, and the fighters themselves.

It was E-Bloc's way, she reminded herself, pressing the civilian population to ensure that they knew very well that they were considered collateral damage. Sun had seen this tactic work a number of times in other developing nations that post-war prosperity had left behind. It was a brutal angle of approach, though it did at times seem to yield results. It was, after all, this same sort of physical oppression that brought an end to the Baltic Spring, and Sun had been lucky to emerge from that conflict with her life.

Sun and her team had been tasked with rooting out the Union and had been standing their digital vigil in staggered shifts ever since the Yakuza operative Takeda had made his final upload.

E-Bloc rampaged across the sector the Asia Prime slingers infiltrated, taking advantage of the sheer chaos unfolding in CodeSource and in the physical realm. Sooner or later they would find evidence of Union operatives, and the struggle for ownership of this island nation's power could begin in earnest.

They were gaining ground again when Hayden Cole logged on. Her organization had plenty of intelligence on the man, though she had never faced him in the datascape before. There was no one else that it could be. He navigated the code with the balance and ease of a seasoned slinger, quickly assessing the source of the problem and bringing down a net to shut them out.

E-Bloc's people, at least those not already booted from CodeSource by the Union slinger's assault code packets, were backing out as fast as they could. Though Cole was coming down hard on both E-Bloc and

Asia Prime slingers, it did not appear that he'd quite realized yet that he was dealing with two different enemies.

It was impossible not to be impressed by the level of skill they exhibited, whoever they turned out to be. This slinger had all the prowess of a digital wage warrior, he had street style, cunning and aggressive in equal measure, making her all the more positive that it was Cole.

There was scarcely time for her to program the tag to fire it off, watching it skate through the code and latch onto his signature. For a moment, she allowed herself to believe that she had succeeded in placing it. The tag followed Cole through a number of municipal systems and leaped from wireless to hardline and back to wireless as the Union slinger shifted his access point over and over. The moment passed, and Sun's heart began to race at the thought that she'd managed it. That he would not see the anomaly in the code, but his sudden pause, half-hidden between rails of streaming symbols, let her know that he had noticed.

He was parked on a civilian server, some entertainment system in the city sector, his momentum halted in the modest device. Her tag was detected, and with it, her chance of an easy win had disappeared. With the tag, she could have, if not brought down the system, then at least gained access to everything the slinger, Cole, had in his files. Near enough to the top of chain that there would likely be something of merit, or at the very least a few clues about how their servers were configured. She had been close. But he was on to her now. And a fight was coming. If he'd intended to dump the tag and run he would have done so already.

Sun straightened her spine, tucked a strand of her dark, chin length, hair behind one ear, careful not to make the jack in the back of her neck shift with the movement. Her equipment was top-notch, but the power grids in this part of the word were temperamental at best. Asia Prime had brought its own remote sources, but that would risk exposure and so was only used at the most important of times. She pulled her fingers from the keyboard for long enough to flex them, to touch the second jack in the back of her neck, before guiding her fingers into the perfect placement. Sun inhaled deeply, allowing the air to fill her lungs from the bottom up, and waited to see what move the Union slinger would make.

E-Bloc was out of this fight, but the new threat was skittering about the code, trying to pin Hayden down with an impressively programmed tag. He was dealing with something different, someone new had jumped in on this action. The more sophisticated tactics and less predictable movements pointed to Asia Prime.

E-Bloc slingers were, in his experience, more likely to do hacks by-the-book, employing classic techniques that, while executed with such skill they were hard to foil, were far easier to see coming.

This slinger was nearly impossible for him to keep up with, and he could not shake the tag. His breathing felt out of rhythm, the hack itself was both exhilarating and exhausting. Hayden's shoulders felt tense and his muscles seemed to tremble. The inside of his cheek slipped back between his teeth without his notice, and he bit down hard, filling his mouth with the taste of copper. No slinger had made him bleed in a long time, Hayden thought, as he regretted not putting in a bit. All the Union slingers had them, as they gave a slinger something to bite down on in moments of intense stress, but they were for rookies.

He felt, at some point, a hand on his shoulder, gentle, grounding pressure.

"C'mon, Hayden."

The voice sounded as though it was filtered through something, like static or leagues of choppy water. The voice lost its inflection on its way to his brain, and he was not sure who it belonged to. Most of the other slingers, and Nibiru, must have pulled out of CodeSource at what they thought was the end of the attack. There was little they could do now, even if they logged back in, some fights were only made more complicated by the presence of other slingers leaving their prints in the code, and he had a feeling this would be one of them.

Besides, he'd stopped running and was parked in a civilian module, so it would take the others several steps to reach him, and if he cut the feed without a proper shutdown procedure he risked extreme nerve damage and brain seizures. Nope, for better or worse, it was time to fight.

As Hayden and the mysterious hacker began to hurl assault and defensive data packets back and forth, making alterations to cause maximum damage, some of the moves employed began to look familiar to him.

Despite the quick, laser-focus of his thoughts, he could recall a reconstruction of a hacking job shown to him in the Asia Prime file. There was still a certain unpredictability that made the moves difficult to counter and push through, but there was little doubt that the hacker was anyone but Sun. She was the leader of all their operations that involved slingers, she was what Hayden was to Union Americana. If you added Nibiru and Overdog to the mixed and pressed that into a single human being that would have been Sun. The best slinger they had on their payroll, who also happened to be a hard systems engineer. And it showed.

She wasn't trying to boot him with simple purge commands or attempting to corrupt his linkup with a virus dump, which is what most slingers would do. Instead, she was intentionally pushing him around, locking him out of hard systems and angling for his core files. It made Hayden think of being a kid and playing keep away with a ball, constantly trying to move around the broken concrete of his hab block while holding onto a faux leather ball that all the other kids were trying to strip from his hands. Sun was coming for him, and she was coming heavy.

A few moves in, he already knew that CodeSource wouldn't cut it. Not with an opponent of this caliber.

She was a master of the hard tech, flawless in her coding. In the face of her immaculate passive assault, Hayden's instinct driven style was being bested at every stroke of the key. In MassNet though, he could get a better feel for who he was fighting, and had a better chance of blocking their attacks before they struck home while launching a few of his own. CodeSource was clearly her battleground, and Hayden needed to lure her into his.

He let his rig carry his consciousness through the reams of code. There was talking behind him again, likely a discussion of what his plan was. He threw up what he hoped was a viable distraction in the code, parked his signature in a local wireless banking ATM, and rapidly went through his shutdown procedures. Hayden's eyes fluttered open, and instantly he knew he'd shut down too hard and too fast for his own good. There was nothing for it, he thought to himself, just have to deal with the pain and push through.

Hayden unhooked the cable from the jack in his neck and stood as quickly as he could make himself, his balance off and the sound in his right ear coming in muffled, as though confused by the sudden change in environment. Normally, the shift out of CodeSource was more gradual, but he could not waste the time.

"Nibiru," he said. She was already behind him. "I need you to hold the space for me. Just until I get back in through MassNet. Don't you dare engage, hear me? That slinger will kill you. If she comes in hot, you run."

She slipped into his chair and immediately plugged her own cable into his mobile rig. The engineer gave him a grin and took a swig from her cooling mug of coffee, sitting it down just as she entered the trance. Hayden hurried across the room, still crowded with panicked personnel. He almost didn't notice Overdog rushing along beside him.

"Please tell me your guys have the throne operational?" Hayden snapped.

"As soon as I realized who it was, I had the lads bring it online. I knew neither of you would let the other go without a fight, you're both famous for that sort of thing." Overdog smiled, his excitement nearly eclipsing the concern spread across his features, before adding, "You've gotta win this kid, or she'll leave you drooling in the throne and have Asia Prime commandos coming through the skylights with bullets for the rest of us."

"I could use a legit challenge, Boss," said Hayden as they walked quickly towards his destination, "Tired of slicing desperate amateurs."

Overdog nodded, and Hayden followed him to a semi-private area, tucked behind a wall that offered the illusion of separateness. More often than not the illusion was all a true slinger really needed. Silence and privacy were nice, but they were not necessities, not when the person doing the slinging was too entangled in the code to even be fully aware of their surroundings.

The throne was much like all the others he had seen, plain, efficient looking, black upholstery where he would be seated. A jungle of wires looped down from the ceiling and the various panels on the surrounding walls. It was lifted just a few feet off the floor, with two tall steps leading up. A helmet with still more wires sprouting from its top was perched atop the headrest.

Hayden looked behind him as he stepped up, watching the attention of the other slingers waver between himself and Nibiru, now fully entrenched in CodeSource.

He sat down, easing his back into the center of the seat and placing his arms and legs in the rests that had been made to hold them. All things considered, it was more comfortable than hunching over his rig at a desk would ever be. He grabbed the twin cables hanging lowest from the apparatus above him and held them between two fingers. He caught Overdog's eye.

"As soon as I'm in, pull Nibiru and fry the board," he said.

Hayden didn't waste time watching the man nod. He was already plugging the first cable and then the second into their respective jacks. He grabbed the helmet and pulled it into place. Almost immediately, his eyes glazed over, and the wall in front of him blurred into black.

MassNet did not appear in columns of constantly shifting code like CodeSource, the symbols and numbers were there, but they stayed just below the surface, sometimes visible and sometimes not, like a ripple on a pond. MassNet appeared as a metaphor for the binary coding experience that was occurring, a backdrop for the action drummed up by the brainwaves of the participants. Scholars still debated over the particulars of whether or not MassNet was a collective hallucination or some kind of non-sentient, hyper-reactive fluid construct that existed in the nebulous datascape generated by a planet full of interconnected systems.

Hayden closed his eyes, blinked to clear away the blur, and a saw a cityscape shaded green with the occasional line of code flickering across the imagined glass of a ground-floor window.

He had seen photographs of Sun scanned into the files about Asia Prime, but they did not prepare him for the sight of the woman in front of him, her form flickering a bit as she abandoned CodeSource for MassNet, having figured out he had made the switch.

She must have had a throne ready, or perhaps, she did all her hacking in one. Hayden knew the exact moment she slotted firmly into this reality because she paused to look at her surroundings; he knew that they would be radically different from what he saw himself.

He watched her face shift into a thin, knife-like smile, before she pulled a gun from the air, from the code, in front of her, and fired it.

In MassNet, you saw what you felt and you felt what you saw. The mind of the slinger taking a back seat to the combined forces of training and instinct. The technique she had employed was just as deadly as a gunshot.

jerked aside as an explosion to his left ripped up the street around him, sending him stumbling sideways, something in his side aching before he could even formulate his own plan of attack. He was not surprised.

Sun was a legend among slingers, her name tossed about and often tacked onto the handles used by up and coming hackers from Asia Prime who had earned their scars under her tutelage.

There were stories about hacks that she had pulled off without a single moment of visible floundering. He did not know the woman he fought, but he knew everything about her history as a hacker. This told him which moves to pull from storage and employ. Sun was good. At least as good as he was when it came down to technicalities and flash, but Hayden had been playing the game longer.

Despite Sun's fearsome reputation, she was barely out of her teens, and he would be willing to bet that he knew more tricks.

Hayden struggled to keep pace with her, rushing closer to slash at her face with a sword that he manifested as he rushed towards her. He missed and his boot.exe cut through non-existent air. Hayden barreled forward, slicing his way through the code, gathering power as he went now that there was little need to be discreet. Even if he tried to take her by surprise, she would spot the ripples in the code and counter whatever attack he had been planning. It was best, in this case, to focus on strength above stealth. He tossed the sword aside and wove a gun of his own.

This was life and death in MassNet, as the throne enabled simultaneous full body immersion and disconnect, enabling the mind in all its glory to rise unfettered from the limitations of the flesh.

When jacked in, the slingers were set free from their bodies and presented with a vast abstraction of cyberspace pulled straight from their own imaginations. Where a civilian might be lost, adrift in a sea of code and iconography, for highly trained slingers it was a semi-coherent world of nearly limitless possibility. While their subconscious mind focused on pushing the envelope of their training on coding and programming language it was their conscious mind that engaged with the visual and auditory metaphor for the binary hard system-based reality that MassNet represented.

Sun watched his angle of attack switch to something easier to see, easier to counter if she could move fast enough. Yet, while the attack was as hard and fast as she expected, more than she'd thought possible, the Union slinger produced a second pistol with his other hand pressed against the small of his back, and the bullet that buried itself below her ribs was unexpected. In the binary world of coding language, the Union slinger had successfully feinted with a telegraphed assault code packet, and while Sun had deftly evaded the first kill.exe she had moved right into the path of the shutdown.exe from his other hand. Cole seemed eager to disconnect her from MassNet, less focused on toasting her, which was not what she'd expected.

The pain was not real, she knew that objectively, but it stole her breath all the same, and what happened in MassNet had a way of carrying over to the real world. If the opportunity to layer imagination and instinct into the discipline of computer science was the blessing of MassNet, then the potential for radical and perhaps even fatal physical harm was the curse. The edges of her rig were beginning to bubble as they fried. Cole's shutdown.exe was heavy duty and high dollar carefully crafted to burn the hard systems and boot Sun's consciousness simultaneously.

Sun cursed, her lips forming the words, but no sound escaping into her silent room, her sanctum. She fired back with just as much heat and more finesse, trying to fry her rival's equipment in turn. The hesitation, the jerking movements before his next attack told her she was at least somewhat successful. Perhaps if she could drop him and melt his hardware the Union would be forced to import another rig. Now that she had at least a modest amount of intel on the Union operation in Manila, she might be able to track the replacement shipment. However, to do that she must not only survive this conflict but emerge as the clear victor.

Sun ducked under a sudden slash from a seemingly razor-sharp battle axe as Cole plowed through the space between them, his previous cunning replaced with the brutality she'd suspected him capable of given his street slinger roots.

Her jack was too hot, the wires inside the cable heating up under the stress. The sheer amount of raw power that was required to simultaneously hold the MassNet simulation and to interact with it was astronomical, and it was taking every spark of power in the base's dedicated system to fuel her cyberspace experience. A dull ache began to twine its way up the column of her spine, driving into her head like a nail through her skull. Sun breathed out a quick, pained gasp, the only sign of her discomfort.

Someone touched the jack, fiddled with the cable briefly to make certain it would hold up, but the outside did not feel as hot as the interior did against her skin. She felt what could only be Hirohito's hands upon her shoulders, somewhere in the distant background of her consciousness, and took comfort in his delicate and yet powerful touch. A sense of calm and resolve spread across her mind and her body and some part of her mind sensed the gentle caress of the alpha augment's fingers upon her flesh.

Hirohito touched her with the intimacy of a lover and the earnestness of a healer, yet there was no sexuality in his ministry, more that he was collaborating with her to mitigate the stress and trauma of her conflict in MassNet. There was a trust between them, and as Sun raised a thin blade to deflect Cole's axe, she found herself reinvigorated.

The slinger's gun arced across the space between them, the streetlights green haze glinting on the dark metal, like moonlight on the surface of a lake. Cole was getting closer, though as he surged forward Sun brought the edge of her blade down across the digital representation of his wrist, and severed his hand from his body.

Suddenly she could see the code changing around him. The gun thudded to the dirt beside her, and she noticed too late that it had changed into a bomb. The hand with the gun had been a baffle.exe, and she'd fallen for it, thinking it was yet another kill.exe or some sort of disconnect protocol.

Her tactics changed to defense, backing out as quickly as she could in hopes of escaping the tag he no doubt hoped to saddle her with amidst the explosion. That's what she would have done. But her feet grew tangled in the thick reams of code as the bomb first emitted what appeared to be a wild growth of vines that encircled her feet before the ordinance detonated. It was a magnificent display of Cole's slinging skills, code-chaining a bramble.exe and a taser.exe in the heat of the moment and successfully deploying the combo after a baffle deployment. She had underestimated this man's sophistication and was paying the price.

The heat and the shock of the explosions buffeted her sideways, and it was only her swift deployment of a retroute.exe that saved her central nervous system, shunting the hard system power spike to one of the many surge protectors affixed to her throne. She lost her footing and when the dust had cleared, found herself on the ground with blood in her mouth and Cole moving closer.

Sun climbed to her feet, ignoring the ache in her chest and the bloodied state of her right arm. In a far-off place, her physical nostrils could smell the acrid stench of melted plastic and burning wires, and she accepted that Cole had likely burned out most of her surge protectors in the deftly executed and deadly feint. She readied the gun she still held, an assault data packet of her own custom design. Cole's foot caught her in her ribs, sending her reeling, but she fired her weapon as she went, burying a bullet in his gut.

Another current shook through her rig into her circuits as she coughed, holding her middle and watching Cole hold his own in turn. She could taste this one, like acid on her tongue. The ache in her head was an earthquake, and the vibrations made her vision blur, the city around them flickering until it was indistinguishable from the landscape of CodeSource.

Each string of code appeared the same as the next, impossible to navigate with any degree of precision. She'd already taken her hands from the keyboard once too often, and could not risk it again. Not when Cole's moves were only growing more confident. She had been slinging long enough to recognize the sight of someone moving in for the kill, long enough to know just how literal that statement could be when applied to this business.

Sun took a chance, closed her eyes until the correct sights rushed back in, and hunkered down behind a pile of the rubble the city was littered with. She manipulated the code that made up her weapon until it grew a longer snout, the pistol turning into a scoped rifle, accurate enough that she could hit Cole in the skull should she find the opportunity for a shot. The crosshairs centered on his face, and she could not help the slight distraction of his hands weaving the code, the focus on his face.

Sun did not realize until she heard the whir of the engine in her left ear, that the rubble was located in the street. Or perhaps she had not started on the street. Maybe he'd moved the street to her. Indeed, she had underestimated the Union slinger, and in her arrogance, had thought to engage him strictly from a first-person shooter perspective. Cole had not only torn apart the insidious.exe she had fired into his guts, but he'd taken their conflict to the next level. He was no longer attacking her directly, but instead using the native code of MassNet itself against her.

It was not an actual truck that rammed into her, she told herself, but that did not make it feel less real. The beast itself had stalled once it struck her, leaving her lying several long yards away. The wall of code in the shape of a vehicle had pummeled her body, and she could not make herself rise.

Her skull felt fractured, the pieces close to shaking apart. The code changed around her. Someone, likely Hirohito, gripped the cable and pulled. The jolt back to consciousness felt like hitting the ground without a parachute, her bones rattling at the jarring sensation of finding herself still in her office.

It was not protocol to un-jack without first powering down, and there would be a cost to her mind and her vitality that would take days to repay, even with help from Hirohito's healing hands, but she had been seconds from overloading, fried into oblivion and left brain-dead, or, if she was luckier, just plain dead. As it was she'd have palsy and night terrors for days, even with treatment.

The Prime slinger powered down her hardware, doing her best to ignore the blood pouring from her nose and knowing that her absence from the datascape would only urge her opponent on. Cole would try that much harder to gain intelligence, perhaps even zero in on her location. The connection severed, Sun removed her helmet and did not contemplate trying to rise from the throne. Already she could hear Hirohito ordering the other slingers to drop melters all along Sun's path through CodeSource and to assault a local banking institution for the purposes of a hard re-direct of the Union's attention.

Sun winked out of existence before he could finish the job. He couldn't help but feel a sense of reprieve at her sudden absence. He'd never had such a hard fight in his life, not in CodeSource, or MassNet, or even in the physical realm. He had not made out so well himself, feeling like he'd been mauled by a freaking bear or something.

He'd done his level best to kill Sun, well aware she'd done the same, even if he'd played on her arrogance and assumed superiority. That was a one time trick and he knew that next time he wouldn't be able to have such an edge, and he knew there would most certainly be a next time.

Killing someone in MassNet would often result in injury of the catastrophic sort. Ruptured capillaries and tertiary nerve clusters, but depending on the quality and depth of penetration of a kill.exe there could be catastrophic damage to the nervous system sometimes death, plain and simple. It had always made him uneasy, and over the years, the disgust had only compounded. One hand pressed to the wound in his middle, Hayden dropped the gun to the ground and watched it fade into the crumbling concrete.

The fight won, the layers of the city around him were rapidly peeling back to reveal nothing but the code he normally saw in CodeSource.

The aftermath of a battle that hard always felt to Hayden like a car wreck. He had won, as far as eliminating the immediate threat was concerned, but he knew, and all the slingers in the room knew too, that Sun was not truly out of the game. Merely sidelined, like he would be if the way he currently felt was any indication. It had been a long time since a fight left him so spent. And, he admitted, a long time since he had faced an opponent of such caliber. He'd had a brush with death, and everyone in the room knew it as well as he did.

Hayden pulled himself back to the forefront of the wall of code, back to where he entered, and set about logging himself out of MassNet and powering down the systems that made the throne tick.

The transition out after such a long stint in the datascape felt gradual if done properly, a slow decline from one plane of reality to another. First, he saw nothing but black inside the helmet. It took him a moment to raise his hands and pull it off. The faces of the slingers around him, of Nibiru and Overdog, were blurred into one, like a messy watercolor. He rubbed a hand over his eyes and reached back with the other one to pull the cables free. He felt lighter without them, but strangely uncomfortable as well, like a soldier without a gun, knowing that attack could come at any time. He tucked it carefully into the pocket of his jacket that was easiest to reach and set about packing up the rest of his equipment. He was running a finger over the melted edge of the computer when sound slotted back into place.

The world around him often came back in stages. This was no surprise.

"—fucking insane," Nibiru was beaming at him. His eyes stuck on the locks of hair poking free from the cap she wore, now pushed halfway back on her head, as though she had tried to run her hand through the messy strands while she watched him work. "You back with us?"

He nodded, let himself grin. He had won this round at least. "Getting there," he answered, head throbbing. It was just shy of painful, blood rushing in his ears and dripping ever so gently from his nose. An ache that he knew was not real, settled into his shoulders and made its way down his back. His fingers twitched. He needed to take his meds and sack out. The sooner he let himself recharge, the sooner he would be back in the game. Meditation was good for resetting the mind and restoring the body after slicing an amateur, but this was something heavier than he could process with meditation. For the first time in years, he needed drugs.

"You got your stuff in your bag?" Nibiru asked.

"Yeah," he answered, trying to be annoyed at the concern, but too tired to find it more than a helpful assurance. Every slinger worth his salt carried something that could knock them out after a hard session. It was dangerous to push your body through a hack of such difficulty, and more dangerous still to ignore the need to heal afterward. It wasn't unheard of for slingers to survive the hack itself, only to push themselves too far afterward, jumping from one long, arduous job into the next.

"How long was it?" He finally got out.

"You're closing in on three hours," she said. "Not the longest I've seen, but you were going at it pretty hard. I know time can seem really condensed in there, but you know what they say, the imagination moves faster than the intellect."

"Just pretty hard?"

She smirked, relaxing at bit at the attempted joke, and lifted one shoulder.

"Yep. I'm not that impressed, to be honest. Seen better."

"Uh huh." He would have rolled his eyes but it was too much effort

Overdog had been standing by, coming closer when Hayden caught his eye. He waited for a congratulatory statement of some sort but was not surprised when it never came. Overdog wanted further instructions to give the group of slingers that surrounded him but was staring at Hayden with something close to awe that made him uncomfortable.

t may have been the aftermath of the hack ripping his brain to shreds, but he felt nothing but irritation at the nothing but irritation at the furious barrage of questions that began to pour out of Overdog a moment later. The manager's questions were white noise for Hayden, like the buzzing of insects in his ears, but like insects they were insistent, and he knew he was going to have to respond somehow.

Overdog was in charge of the operations of the Union's hackers for a reason, but sometimes, the man's lack of social graces was downright appalling.

"Just fix the damage for now," he said, cutting off the man in the midst of a string of questions. "I have to crash, and I'd really like to find a room with a mattress before I do it here. I have one, upstairs I think, it's nice."

At his back, gathering her things, Nibiru snorted. "I'll carry your stuff," she offered. "The extra ten pounds might do you in."

He didn't have the breath to deny it and figured there was a fairly good chance she was right anyway.

Overdog seemed cowed enough that he left Hayden be, and set about trying to preach his plan of action to the group of slingers that were still, for the most part, staring at Hayden as he made his way to the door, taking quick, measured steps. His knees felt ready to give way. He should have known this was going to be a hard one, just taken care of it in his room, where, when he was finished, he could have walked the two steps from the desk to the bed and collapsed in the mess of blankets.

Nibiru was close behind him, her own bag over one shoulder, still clumsily shoving Hayden's things into his own. She held up the half-melted rig.

"Guess I'll have to trash that," he said.

"You could always sell it to one of your new groupies," she suggested, jerking her head back at the handful of slingers watching them leave.

Despite the growing pain his skull, he snorted a laugh, let her push open the door and hold it for him.

He wondered how much experience she had with the end-of-a-bender feeling that took over after a hack that intense. They wouldn't have assigned her to him as backup if she did not, Hayden figured, however good she was with her engineering gig. She seemed to know to keep the conversation light and easy to follow, only requiring the barest of answers from him in return.

She steered him away from the room that held his private workspace and toward the elevator, hitting the button for their floor and then stepping back to let him walk on ahead of her.

Laine, on her way out, nearly bowled him over in her haste to reach her destination. Normally, her cybernetics would have prevented such a mistake, but her expression, for once, was more rushed than focused. They must have pulled her off whatever job she'd been assigned to for this. Her head tilted as she steadied him with a hand on his shoulder, and as she caught the dead tired, satisfied look on his face, her mouth formed the off-kilter smile he was familiar with.

"The official reports claim it was Sun. Was she as good as her reputation would indicate?"

He scarcely had the energy to make himself smile back, but if Laine had drummed one up for him, it was the least he could do. "Better," he said. "But not quite as good as me."

"So says the dead man," Nibiru muttered, though she gave Laine a friendly enough nod.

"I'm glad," Laine replied. She let go of his shoulder, and he nearly stumbled again without the weight of it holding him steady. She exited the conversation with that, hitting the button to close the doors as she passed and continuing down the hallway.

Hayden kept one side glued to the wall, fingers curled around the cold metal of the railing until the elevator came to a stop. Nibiru waited until then to break the silence that had settled. Laine had been focused, very focused in fact. Hayden had seen her like that before. Things were about to get rather colorful if he knew Laine as well as he thought he did.

"She seems nice enough," Nibiru confided. "And I'm all for advancements in cybernetics. But she kind of freaks me out. What about you?"

Hayden took a weary step forward. It was easier once he got going, like riding a bike. "Laine's...kind of a lot." He spoke slowly, words careful. He found Laine as unnerving as the next person, but he had known her a while and a certain sense of loyalty made him curb his tongue. "You get used to it, and when she's around nothing can touch us. I'm glad she's on our side."

Nibiru huffed. "Yeah," she said. "Me too I guess."

His room was just ahead. He had to fumble for his card for too long but eventually dug it free from the grip of his deep front pocket. The door opened, Nibiru followed him inside, but only long enough to hand over his bag and watch him dig through it for the meds that would put him under.

A special blend of nerve chemicals put together by Americana for its slingers. You could get the stuff without corporate connections; he'd even bought it on the street a few times when he was just starting out, barely better than the freelancer he'd faced the previous week, but you took a risk scoring balance pills from just anyone. It was an easy formula to screw up. Too much of the wrong thing and you never woke up. Too little and you woke up on the wrong end of a seizure.

He shook out the recommended dosage, this was one area in which he normally stuck to protocol, and downed the pills dry, with Nibiru watching.

"Guess I'll catch you in 18 hours," he said. The pills worked fast, the sleep they brought on nearly instantaneous, giving you just enough time to find the nearest flat surface and collapse. He could very well have taken them downstairs, but he was certain that having a slinger asleep in the middle of a busy floor for that long counted as a breach of fire code, or maybe just Overdog's misplaced sense of professionalism.

"Buzz me if you're dying," she said, flipping off the light as she neared the door, tugging her hat back into its proper position.

His vision grayed out just as he heard the door close.

6

Cole looked like shit, but that was to be expected if he had gone up against a slinger as formidable as Sun. After such a long stint in MassNet, he would likely be out of commission for a solid day at least, leaving the protection of the system and the continued search for the signal emanating from the energy source in the hands of those less skilled in cyberwarfare.

Laine was significantly disappointed about that bit, though she begrudgingly admitted that it was a necessary sacrifice. If Hayden didn't rest, he would be no good to anyone, least of all the Union's mission here. At least there was the engineer.

Nibiru was a top-notch Union agent despite her lack of hostile operations experience, of that Laine was sure, having been asked to look over the woman's records before the final decision to hire her on had been made. Laine disliked the prospect of going into the field without Cole looking over her shoulder from the digital realm.

Overdog might be over the hill as a slinger, but he excelled in pushing his staff to feats of greatness if they had it in them. She doubted, however, based on their prior performance against the combined assault of E Bloc and Asia Prime, that Overdog's cadre had much in them for the old slinger to push. Laine admitted that her standards were high, based on her years working and fighting alongside Cole, but she trusted the plucky engineer to hold things steady in the digital realms until Hayden was back in the game. She told herself these things as she prepared to depart, a convenient narrative to justify abandoning the HQ for a short time in order to pursue her own endeavors.

Laine scarcely checked in on the commotion among the slingers before heading out. This was not an authorized trip away from HQ, but her level of clearance allowed her to go where she liked without harassment from security, even if they actually logged her exit and re-entry to the facility. There would be a reckoning upon her return if she didn't come back with results. The job was like that sometimes, encouraging individual operative to take risks, though without results the transgressions would be frowned upon.

They simply assumed she wouldn't risk breaking protocol on such an instrumental mission, not realizing that Laine would do whatever she thought necessary, the corporation's suffocating rules notwithstanding. Sometimes there were advantages to having much of her service record hidden away from the general staffers by several layers of security clearance. She knew it was a tactical risk to enter hostile territory without a slinger watching over her, though she had not yet established sufficient trust with Nibiru to ask the young engineer for an assist.

It looked like she was breaking the rules on her own this time, and Laine couldn't help but find some degree of excitement in that. Without an ally to be her eyes and ears, to clear a path through the world and close it behind her again, the alpha augmented warrior would truly be on her own.

Mitchell, himself, had told her that one of his security teams was already in the process of investigating the Akiaten who had attacked the E-Bloc troopers, going local in plainclothes and for her not to concern herself.

Laine trusted the soldiers and security goons to investigate, to find what information there was on the surface and report back. Their job was an investigation and site security, while Laine was meant to be deployed only in the most dire of circumstances, something of the nuclear option from a human resources perspective.

Laine was not at all content to remain inactive, it was an insult to the hardware she had given up a portion of her humanity to bear. These Akiaten intrigued her and she wanted to track them to their source herself, to experience the thrill of the hunt firsthand. If she ran into trouble with E-Bloc troopers looking for the same, then it simply gave her an excuse to eliminate a few of them while she was at it. Laine was not averse to fun, she just liked to make her own, and there wasn't a doubt in her mind that Basilica knew she would do something like this. In fact, she was positive that the brash executive had every expectation of just this sort of behavior from of Cole and herself.

Even with the sun going down, the air outside HQ was a sweltering miasma, and she was glad of the change from the generally pleasant atmosphere in New LA. It made things feel, to her, just a touch more pressured. As if the weight in the air synced with the gravitas of the mission itself, giving her a tactile reminder of the risks present and the rewards at stake.

The sun still needed to crawl a few inches lower to bring the city to full dark, but Laine had no trouble picking her way through the civilians that lingered on the sidewalks. She had the hood of the moisture resistant long coat pulled over her head, and with her blonde hair pushed back behind her ears, there was little of her distinctive features visible in the long shadows of growing night.

The locals mostly walked in small throngs, heading to the bus station or the bar she had glimpsed a few blocks over, though always in groups, as was customary in such troubled places in the world. The tension was palpable, and it reminded Laine of other clandestine war zones and places of clashing corporate interests and civil unrest.

She saw one lone woman, dark hair swinging with her steps as she walked around a corner with a backpack slung over one shoulder, but she was the only person Laine glimpsed alone. The still image that Laine snapped of the woman with her ocular mod was of only marginal use, as the woman's face was all but obscured by her hair and the high collared coat she wore. However, height, weight, and gait estimates would provide useful datapoints if ever the image and accompanying two seconds of video were needed for identification purposes.

The operative made her way two blocks over, to where both Mitchell's report and the hacked and re-hacked traffic cams told her the

Akiaten had appeared from. She moved her eyes from one street to the next, following the path they would have taken.

The car that the E-Bloc troopers had used for cover had been hauled away, but she knew exactly where it had set, and upon walking there, saw the gold glint of a spent bullet casing wedged between two breaks in the sidewalk. Thanks to the synthetic neural net upgrades she'd endured which allowed her brain to rapidly process the mountains of data her augmented senses pushed upon her, little escaped her scrutiny.

She bent to pull it free, feeling the rough bent edge of the casing with the pad of one finger, fighting off the urge to push harder and feel her blood well up around the inevitable cut. She tucked the shell into a pocket and walked on, tracing the path the Akiaten had taken upon their retreat, down a small side street and out of the view of both Hayden (from the alley he had claimed to be standing in) and the security camera footage.

The road here had crumbled so severely that it was closer to gravel that anything resembling asphalt or concrete. Such were many of the streets Laine had walked down in the world outside the glittering cities of Union Americana, where progress had all but halted and the natural forces of entropy paired with municipal neglect. There were scuffs in its surface, obvious places where it had been disturbed by harder than casual footfalls, but enough time had passed now that it would be next to impossible to discern the difference between the prints of the Akiaten and anyone else who happened to cut through. It looked to be a popular shortcut for anyone on the run from one block to the next.

Laine tapped her temple twice with her index fingers, pulling up the enhanced vision she often used when tracking became necessary. In the blink of an augmented eye, she felt the additional load strain upon her neural net as the ocular mods increased their sensitivity to a level that would have burned out her brain had she not endured the neural upgrades to match the oculars.

Bascilica had asked her a thousand times not to rely overmuch on those mods, as they were honestly designed for advancing canine units more than they were human beings, but as far as Laine was concerned, this was exactly the sort of situation in which using it was paramount. Learning more about their enemies was of the utmost importance, and anytime she spent stumbling looking for clues, perhaps in the wrong direction completely, would be time lost that they could not afford, not with both Asia Prime and E-Bloc to contend with in addition to this new threat from the locals.

As soon as her vision focused again, she looked back at the loose mix of dirt and rock under her feet, now able to pick out the individual prints, how old they were, and which sets matched with others. Her impossibly elevated sensory awareness even detected tiny specs of blood upon the crumbling street as she crossed from one to the next. The trail was rust-red, but the faded drops looked bright as paint through her eyes.

She followed the boot prints and the spilled blood. When the trail became muddled once more, a fork in the road slowing her progress, she employed her other senses as well. Small tubes inserted in her nostrils that lead back to a small processor in her nasal cavity decoded the scents around her. With everything on, she could follow what she could see, but also other, deeper things, like sweat, the residue that gunpowder left behind, both of them sharp in her nose, new enough that she wondered if they used this same path often.

She followed the scattered remnants of the trail to the outskirts of the city; they were already situated close to its edge, and it was not a long trip.

With the sun going down, the number of people on the street this far from the district center thinned drastically. It was easy to keep on track without going out of her way to avoid being sighted, and thus far not a single E Bloc trooper had crossed her path. That was odd, considering the recent conflicts, though she was so focused on the hunt that she let the detail slip away into the tumble of data from her senses.

The grass grew tall here, springing up through the cracks in the sidewalk, a deep green much richer than the yellowed, dry stuff that grew in her own city.

The encroaching darkness made it hard for her instruments to track the blood, especially when the amount began to wane drastically, as though the wound had been bound. Perhaps the culprit had taken a different route and she missed the exact moment when he veered away from the direction of the others, though such an oversight was unlikely given her heightened augmentations.

She stopped, leaned one shoulder against the trunk of a tree while she cranked up the specs on her sensors, placing the focus on scent. She was starting to get a headache and Laine knew she was pushing her neural augments to the limit. With the miracle of cyberware, an alpha augment could mimic the sensory prowess of dogs and wolves, though it could only be done for a short time before the human mind, which had not evolved to process so much raw sensory data, was overburdened. Even with the upgrades, Laine was on the bleeding edge of what was possible, and soon the cost to her body would come due if she did not ease up on the throttle of her augments. Regardless of the lack of blood or the impossibility of picking prints out among the tall grass, if she could keep to the scent trail, she should manage to stay on track.

With the specs on her equipment tweaked, the smells were easier to pick up on and to differentiate. She noted what she had missed before, there was a smell deeper than the gunmetal or the sweat that followed after a firefight, something that seemed to be the Akiaten themselves. The aroma was both slight enough and strange enough that even her advanced instruments were barely registering it. Her equipment should have been capable of recognizing anything, and as long as she had used it, it had. The 'UNKNOWN' that cropped up beside it in her heads-up display, the HUD, meant one of two things: she was experiencing her first technical failure since working for Union Americana, or, it was something new. Just one more confounding detail about the Akiaten to file away.

Laine pulled up a view of the scent signature and saved it to her files. Once she knew more, once she finished tracking, she would send it along to Bascilica and let him decide where the knowledge would do the most good.

The fact that her hardware did not recognize the scent, thankfully, did not make it any less easy to follow with her specs cranked up. There wasn't a clean break between the city and the jungle. The transition was gradual, and Laine found herself walking through a mix of tall grass and scattered gravel, buildings still in sight at her back. She crossed an old, abandoned set of railroad tracks, her enhanced vision telling her that nothing had ridden the rails in years. She scuffed her boot against the line of iron within the wood, there were newer ones within the city's center she knew, a metro that ran from one end of the city to the next. She wondered what other things lay forgotten this far out. It seemed to her as if the jungle itself was reaching out to reclaim parts of the city left decayed by neglect.

Laine followed the scent trail through the grass, the scattering of trees, and over a creek small enough for her to simply step across with one long stride. It wound its way through the landscape as far into the distance as her vision could track.

There were few buildings out this far, but she glimpsed several as she followed the trail. An old trailer, more rust than metal, all but one of its windows broken. What looked to have once been an old apartment block rested in the midst of some swampy ground. The brick on one side was painted blue, but the paint had long since begun to chip away.

She circled, briefly abandoning the trail to look at it from all sides. The windows were in better shape, and someone had draped a tarp in front of the hole where the front door used to stand. She wouldn't have been surprised to find someone squatting inside it. The last neighborhood she passed through had been less than pristine, but this one was in full urban decay and positively radiated a sort of malice that set her teeth on edge. She had crossed a threshold, and was in some nebulous in-between-space, an unseen border between the order of civilization and the chaos of anarchy.

The sun sank the last few inches toward the earth, dipping below the buildings on the horizon and plunging her world further toward full dark.

Activating another sensor with a tap of her finger to the right part of her skull, the trail that the Akiaten left became something corporeal, the datapoints plotted and illuminated by her HUD, a line of shimmering silver that she could follow with her eyes.

As the trees grew closer together, the remaining light dropped away, making her cybernetics all the more necessary. Laine walked softly. Her armor, were Americana's funds less than impressive, might have weighed her down, made her movements slower and her footprints easy to see even for people without their own enhancements. As it was, her armor was sturdy, but light and her feet were practiced enough that they scarcely made a sound even when they trod over dry branches and twigs.

She had walked scarcely a mile further, scant moonlight filtering down through the trees, when she saw the trail disappear around the corner of a single-level house in a neighborhood that had all but been swallowed up by the encroaching jungle foliage.

It was in better shape, structurally than any of the other buildings she had passed since leaving the city, and that fact alarmed her, causing the alpha augmented warrior to gently rest a hand upon the grip of her automatic pistol, snugly holstered upon her thigh.

The windows and doors were intact, the siding a faded yellow. The only indication of its abandoned status were the vines that hung down from the roof, crawling their way over the dusty window glass, curving toward the sill as though trying to force it open.

She used both the trees and her own silence for cover as she crept closer, knees slightly bent to accommodate a crouch in case someone should open the door, or a flash of movement appeared in the window.

It was true that she was here to disrupt their operations, perhaps capture one of their soldiers for interrogation if it was a viable possibility, but before she did, it would be best to find out whatever she could by watching and waiting. Surveillance was a crucial part of any reconnaissance operation, and at its core, that was all this was. While she genuinely hoped for a challenge worthy of her lifetime of augmentations, this was neither the time nor the place.

She engaged the shimmer effect of her heavy coat, sending electrical signals through the delicate circuitry of the lining that activated the previously inert micro-panels affixed to the surface of the coat. The panels were only a square millimeter in size, machine stitched into the fabric, and once activated they would reflect her surroundings, allowing her to use the coat as camouflage that worked well enough so long as she wasn't actively moving. With it, Laine had sat in dark corners and shadowed stairwells for hours unnoticed, zeroing in on the conversations that went on around her and recording anything relevant with her audio implants to send back to HQ, wherever it happened to be.

Twenty minutes passed, and yet she heard nothing but cicadas and the distant crunch of leaves. Her senses still in overdrive, it was easy to tell that the sound was made by animal rustling in the leaves rather than one of her targets. The house was empty or its occupants were dead. With her cybernetics configured to pick up strange scents, she had no doubt she would have smelled the decay if that were the case. Of course, there was still a chance that more of their group would show up or return, and she risked being caught in the house, which appeared to have only one exit.

Laine stood and smiled, wider than normal since there was no one to see it. If they came then they came, and she would relish the chance to see them in a fight without the lens of a camera coloring her view of the action.

Laine was careful as she had been trained to be, her handgun already drawn and ready to fire. Her rifle rested between her shoulder blades, in case she had need of it, her blade hung at her right hip, the hilt bumping the inside of her arm when she moved it the right way, a reassurance. Even as good a sniper as she was, guns had failed her before. She had had no such trouble with swords.

Laine's hand felt too heavy for the small, rusted doorknob, but it opened easily enough and sustained no damage. She filed away this curiosity, having expected to kick down the door, or, if such a hovel had reinforcements, to force her way through the lock with some of her equipment.

The interior was dark and dusty as she expected, but she saw it clearly enough with her cybernetics still enhancing the view. The headache had subsided, pushed to the back of her awareness by the surge of adrenaline coursing through her as she entered the building ready for a fight.

It boasted several mildewed couches and chairs, and a long, wooden table with an array of seating in what looked to be the kitchen. One of the chairs had only three legs and had been left discarded in a corner.

She was surprised to find that the electricity worked when she flicked a switch, bathing the house in a jaundiced, yellow glow. She'd seen no wiring and the power lines didn't stretch this far. They must have been siphoning from the grid somehow, but that wasn't her area of expertise. She made another note, sure that someone at HQ could do something with the information, even if she gleaned nothing else from this visit. CodeSource might not get the slingers very far out here, but if the house was still on the grid somehow, they'd find a way in.

Upon further searching, she discovered two small bedrooms, both of which were occupied by several mattresses, some with actual beds to hold them up, but most without. She counted seven, not including the two sleeping bags she dragged her feet over in the back end of the shadowed hallway. These looked slept in. Most interestingly, under one of the beds, she found an array of melted computer equipment, similar to the disposable rigs that criminal underworld and freelance slingers were fond of. Even she could tell that they were destroyed too thoroughly to extract anything from, but she photographed the state of them regardless. The make of their chosen technology might be relevant to any counter attacks that Overdog set up with Hayden. These had the hallmark of freelance rigs, so perhaps the source of the parts they'd been built from could be investigated.

She crossed her fingers for a hidden door, a tunnel to an underground compound, something to make the trip seem worthwhile, but a second examination of the house led to no further discoveries aside from a few half-empty boxes of bullets in one of the kitchen drawers. She pocketed a few out of habit, though likely there was little to be gained from examination of them. They were .223 field rounds, which would have been an item of interest if they hadn't been low-end gamma loads, indicating that they were refurbished from scavenged civilian model casings, with homemade alloy tips, and likely intended for hunting bush meat. If used against modern combat armor gammas tended to just flatten on impact with little damage to the target. The place had been stripped clean, and if the recently used bedding was any indication, it had not been done long ago. She cursed herself for not hitting the streets as soon as Cole was back with the food and intel, long before the late-night code fight. The precious hours she'd lost had given them plenty of time to exfil.

Laine kicked the melted tech beneath the bed and headed for the main room. She had just left the narrow hallway when the first of the bullets screamed out of the darkness towards her. Her enhanced senses picked up the noise and magnified it to a deafening roar for a moment before the internal dampeners flatlined the auditory assault.

Laine shut down her over-cranked augments quickly, automatically, but the damage was done. She was left with one ear, the one angled toward the front door, that would not cooperate and a dizzy, off feeling in her head. While the cyberware would be fine, there was likely a rupture in her eardrum. An easy fix from the med station once she returned to HQ, but for now, it was painful and she had to actively shunt the biofeedback from the injury.

In the base of her neck, at the back, was a small capacitor that was plugged into her lower brain, the primitive parts that governed the most basic of bio-functionality in the human body. With the right neural upgrades, which she had, the electrical signals that communicated pain from the injured part of the body to the brain could be temporarily, but instantly, re-directed to the capacitor. So long as she did not overload the machine, Laine could potentially suffer a great many injuries before actually having to consciously cope with the trauma.

Adrenaline poured into her veins, making her vision sharper and her movements smooth and quick, made all the more so by the upgrades to her musculature and skeletal structure.

More rounds tore through the house, and given the shifting trajectories, she estimated that there were at least three or more shooters, all moving in a circular pattern around the house while firing inwards. A smile crept across her face as the guilty pleasure of furious combat overcame the professional embarrassment of having been successfully bushwhacked by unknown assailants.

With blinding speed, Laine raised her automatic pistol and squeezed the trigger as she twisted her waist and swept her right leg in a wide arc, keeping the point of her boot on the floor as she pivoted on the ball of her right foot. She ended the spin in a crouching position, having sprayed the contents of the extended magazine, eighteen rounds in total, in a three-hundred-and-sixty-degree circle. While it was highly unlikely that she'd hit any of the assailants, the fusillade would make it nearly impossible for the enemy to pinpoint her position from outside while also ducking for cover. She'd bought herself a few precious moments and she holstered her now empty pistol so that she could make the best of them.

The largest couch, situated directly adjacent to the front window, made good cover, even if just to disrupt any low-grade scopes that might be picking up on heat signatures or abundant movement.

She ducked behind it as she grabbed her rifle and thumbed off the safety after powering down the armor sync. Most of her augments were internal, giving off negligible digital or heat signatures, though the cables leading from her skull, just behind her ear, that connected her HUD to the armor, had to be cut cold. The enemy obviously knew someone was inside the building, though possibly they did not know, as of yet, just who they'd caught in their net, and perhaps the alpha augment could use that fact to her deadly advantage.

She half crawled to the windows, a smirk on her lips, barely making a sound against the old wood floor, holding her weight in her arms and the balls of her feet as she moved. She did not need a rest for her gun, she was more than strong enough and skilled enough to hold it steady, but she placed it in the open window anyway because it was an opportune spot. There were shadows dancing through the trees, firing bullets at the house haphazardly, the uncoordinated attempts letting her know that they still had no pinpoint on her position. They only knew there was someone inside. As fully as she had let her guard down once inside the house, they had likely seen her movements through the glass.

She tuned out the sound of gunfire, not an insignificant feat, even for those accustomed to lives of violence, and stole a quick glimpse through her scope. The bit of the jungle the scope showed her included a soldier kneeling with his rifle pressed into the crook of his shoulder.

Was it her augments or her instinct that had encouraged her to sight upon this exact spot of jungle? She cared little for the answer, and it was only her lack of concern that gave her pause, even if just for the millisecond it took to register with her.

The second thing she noticed was the E-Bloc armor that covered him, and presumably the rest of the squad firing rounds into the house. The bullets stopped moments later, and she lowered her gun, wary of one of them spotting the glint of her weapon or the moonlight catching the glass of her scope.

She could tell they were communicating on a self-contained band, the interference of their system making audio snow in her mind as she tested the frequencies in an attempt to unsuccessfully pick up on their squad channel.

If Hayden had been riding shotgun in CodeSource for this op he could have raided their hardware by jumping the grid and coming at them through their own broadcast, but without him, she had no way of listening in. The building had been sprayed with bullets, but no alarm had been sounded and no one had rushed out the single exit in a panic.

They were thinking the same thing she was, that the place was empty of living beings. She'd thought it was a result of flight, but they were basing their judgments on a lack of activity or sensor pings because they were sure nobody survived their punishing fire.

It wasn't an unfair assessment, as Laine knew that her armor had registered no less than four hits, and though the stout armor had held, her pain capacitor was nearly exhausted from the concussive trauma of so many impacts.

Any competent military operation though would have to confirm that before calling it done. All kills had to be confirmed. They would send a few men forward, perhaps a team of two, while the rest sat back and waited. Even without her hearing working properly, it was still enough to count the sets of footsteps. She knew that at least two were making their approach.

It took the two soldiers less than a minute to reach the door from the place they had fired, and when they walked inside, their eyes flitted right over her, safely ensconced in the shadows between the rightmost arm of the couch and a table that held a small lamp.

Her shimmer coat did its job. Thankfully the energy signature of the coat was so subtle that the sensors would have to be right on top of her to notice, and by then it would be too late. The only way to beat the shimmer was with the naked human eye. Most digital systems could be baffled, and when the coat was combined with competent analog stealth techniques, detection was difficult indeed.

"They've got a power hookup, somehow," one of the men said in a thick E Bloc accent, looking at the flickering, naked bulb above the kitchen sink, "Off grid but not tied to a local generator like they've got a ghost grid set up somewhere."

They were not below par soldiers, their thoughts turned the same way her own did. They skirted through the kitchen and moved down the hallway, each man covering the other as they moved. E Bloc had sent seasoned troops to these islands, and that fact gave Laine some satisfaction in the expectation of a legitimate challenge.

The opportunity Laine awaited had arrived. She rose from her crouch, leaving her rifle on the floor, and drawing the blade from her side. She set the telescoping blade to extend twelve inches to make it more effective in the close quarters of the hallway.

After the leader of the two had turned into the first bedroom to investigate, she silently killed the one who lagged behind., having set the telescoping blade to extend twelve inches to make it more effective in the close quarters of the hallway, the sword slipped quickly into the line of his spine, severing the cord and bringing him to his knees with no more sound than a quick exhaled breath of shock.

The second soldier fell just as quickly, her blade slicing through his throat from behind, blade extended to twenty-two inches, his heels drumming on the floor while his blood leaked out and slipped through the spaces between the old boards. Knowing she might not have the same chance with the soldiers outside, she took a quick video of the man's death—the struggling, gurgling sound that faded gradually into silence. Laine left the bodies where they fell, and made her way back to the window, hands aching for the weight of her rifle to fill them.

She did a quick sweep, counted five, and lined up the first target in her scope. Thinking they'd hemmed in the threat, the troopers had formed up as a squad, a standard assault pattern, in preparation of moving in on the house.

For all the advantage they'd had at the outset, they'd given it up in their confidence of having killed their opponent in the opening salvo and sending two men to finish the job if, in fact, she'd still been alive. The first man wore no helmet, as did two of the others, and it was easy to send a bullet through the middle of his forehead. His brains splattered messily along the greenery behind him and though she wished for a picture of that as well, there was no time to waste.

Her next kill almost matched, just a bit to the left of the center and down, as the man started to stand during her shot, a reflexive reaction to the explosion of blood and bone beside him. The remaining three were running forward, firing wildly at the house instead of scrambling for cover.

Laine had experienced this tactic in the past, a standard E Bloc response pattern. While it might have seemed to the untrained eye as a suicidal rush into the enemy's guns, the alpha augment knew better from experience. The firepower unleashed by the troopers was impressive, and against conventional opponents, it would have driven the enemy back. Unfortunately for the troopers, Laine was anything but conventional. She had long ago had several neural augmentations implemented that managed her fear response.

As bullets tore into the wood of the house, sending splinters into her face and neck, Laine did not flinch, nor did she look away from the task at hand. As more rounds ripped through the walls and pounded against her armor the Union warrior held her aim steady and squeezed the trigger.

She felled one of the troopers with a shot to his middle, the high-powered round piercing his thick combat armor at the seam where his torso met his waist, sending him sprawling into the dirt of the jungle floor. A second trooper fired a wide spray of bullets, never breaking stride as he advanced under fire, shattering the windows further and peppering the outside of the house with holes.

Laine didn't bother chambering another round in the heavy rifle. It was peerless in its ability to penetrate even the stoutest of infantry grade combat armor, but it was a clumsy beast in the close quarters fighting that was about to erupt.

She slid the pistol from its holster, rushing towards the door, slapping a fresh magazine into the bottom of the weapon and silently admonished herself for neglecting to reload as soon as the first mag went dry. The duel with Takeda's samurai bodyguard had awakened something in her apparently, a need so strong it overwhelmed her formerly immaculate battle discipline, and it hungered for hand to hand combat. She stayed to one side of the door, swiftly powering up her armor sync so that she could re-route all the energy to her front in anticipation of the firefight to come.

Seconds later, when the trooper reached the entrance and shoved the muzzle of the gun through, she stepped forward grabbed it. Her fingers closed around the heated barrel and drove it back and up, smacking the butt of the weapon into her assailant's helmet visor with savage intensity. She pressed the barrel of the pistol against his now exposed throat and sent a round through his windpipe while he was still stumbling backward, trying to right the weapon in his hands.

The last man ran.

Laine stepped over the man she'd left dying on the ground and switched to full auto.

The trooper was sprinting towards the treeline. Laine raised her pistol to track his movement and activated her auditory recorder. She shot him in the back as he fled. The first fourteen rounds stripped away the armor protecting his neck and shoulders and drove him to his knees, the last four tunneled into his exposed flesh.

The thump of his body sounded different on the soft, grassy earth, a peculiar new sound that Laine had yet to experience, and she was happy for having the foresight to capture it. She walked over to him, hoping to watch the dying man's light leave his eyes, but he was already gone when she reached him.

She returned to the house briefly, to snap more stills of the two men she'd killed inside as if discovering their staffing profiles would make any difference. She shut the door behind her, and marked the coordinates in her files; she would need a team to come out and dispose of the bodies. Mitchell would be pissed, but snuffing a squad of E- Bloc troopers weren't the worst outcome, and perhaps there was more to this encounter than she'd initially considered, especially in light of this sudden and violent conflict.

The logistics behind the entire encounter confused her, now that she'd had time to send in her coordinates and flush the adrenaline from her system. The trail had been clear, the Akiaten had used the place, possibly up till only mere hours before she'd arrived. And the appearance of E-Block just as she was preparing to leave seemed too convenient. She hung her rifle back over her shoulder and walked back through the trees. One possibility loomed above the rest, that the Akiaten had known she would track them here, and had tipped off E-Bloc themselves.

Instead of the irritation she had expected to accompany the thought, she merely felt impressed. A challenge had been issued, with bold intent and perfect clarity now that she was aware of the signs of the firefight's orchestration. She felt recklessly eager to meet that challenge, and her estimation of the enemy was elevated with a respect only matched by her growing desire to eliminate them.

7

Most slingers, when faced with such a recent, near death experience, would give into the urging of their body to take the prescribed drugs and sleep.

Sun was not most slingers.

As with most problems that presented themselves for her solving, she had her own solution. The hacker drugs were marketed by the pharmaceutical corporations and bought up by anyone who employed slingers. While there might be a modest variety among the medications, they were all meant to achieve the same end result. Sometimes, for those slingers not working on the record, there were other, less legal means of obtaining such drugs, but that usually meant the drugs themselves were less safe, made by amateur chemists in their basements, crucial ingredients thinned with something else to cut down on the cost. When you bought equilibrium on the black market, you were risking more than just your money.

That wasn't a problem with the drugs issued so generously by Asia Prime. Sun had no doubt that the product they handed out to each slinger on the payroll was top of the line. She simply didn't like them, the drugs, that is. There was little way to regulate how long they knocked you out for, as every person's body was different, and despite Asia Prime's deep pockets even they were not in a position to spend the kind of fortunes it would require to tailor a pharmaceutical to an individual slinger, especially if that slinger might get burned on the very next hack. As a result, one had to assume that close to a day would be lost regardless of how much rest your body actually needed.

Sun knew exactly how many hours her brain needed to recharge. She did sleep, but it was not the chemically induced coma brought on by the equilibrium drugs. She simply left the throne immediately after the attack, debriefed her superiors on what had occurred and had herself checked out by the on-call staff in the medical wing, before finding a bed and laying down. It was an easy thing to give into the exhaustion that had settled into her bones during the hack, to hunker down in a pile of blankets and pillows for a handful of hours before her alarm forced her back to wakefulness. It was a nap and nothing more, nothing close to the hard sleep enforced by the meds.

Even so, her head felt muddled, thoughts catching in spider-webs as they bounced around her skull. Sun settled down on a soft mat that rested in front of the wide, floor to ceiling window of her room, sitting with her legs crossed in the spot of afternoon sunlight. The hack had been this morning and had lasted almost to noon. The clock on her phone told her it was a quarter 'til two.

She let herself slip into a meditative state, her consciousness winding down from the quick-paced, frantic dreams she'd suffered in her bed. Her mind was still panicked by the close call in the data-scape. Her brain was still processing information much faster than it needed to now that she was unplugged, stuck in flight or fight mode with no way to ease down. No way but this.

Sun slowed her breathing down, felt the stress unwind from each muscle. The tight band of worry cinched around her ribs fell away, and the headache still pounding away behind her eyes started draining away with each breath. Her fingers drummed on her knees, before dropping to her sides, tension in her shoulders loosening. She stayed there for a long time, her body and her mind entering together, the relaxed, trance-like state they always found.

This was a renewal that went deeper than simple sleep, a delving into the core of her being that released the stress and fatigue that had knotted in her body and in her mind. When she felt herself begin to resurface, she was always tempted to let herself drift even further away, to stay in the space where not even her own thoughts could pester her too much. The monks called those rampant thoughts 'monkey mind', the constant chattering of the mind's inner voices that needed to be continuously silenced in order to achieve the balanced state.

She would have remained in this place of no-mind for much longer, but there were things that needed her attention, first of all, her own growling stomach. Slingers burned through thousands of calories when they were inside MassNet, and she could feel her hands tremble ever so slightly. She had not eaten since the early hours of the morning, while watching E-Bloc's progress from afar, as they hacked into the Union Americana mainframe, using the distraction of their efforts as a window to slip in through.

As she meditated, she had felt the warmth of the sun slowly dissipate, and so, before she even let her eyes open into slight slits, she knew the sun had gone down.

She opened them slowly, letting them adjust to the scant light left over in her quarters. When she stood, her knees popped. She rolled her shoulders and stretched, rose up onto the balls of her feet before sinking back down, resting her heels on the plush carpet.

It was impressive really, what a grand job the corporation had done as far as fixing the place up went. An amusing thought struck her, that the nice new structures built by the warring corporations to fight this war would be the only things left standing in a sea of rubble by the time this conflict had achieved its ordained resolution. Perhaps it was not the sort of thing that would be amusing to the average person, but Sun allowed herself a chuckle as she changed into a fresh set of clothes and ran her fingers through her hair until it looked passable enough. One had to find amusement where one could, especially on these deep runs that took operatives like her quite far from the pleasantly suffocating embrace of Asia Prime corporate culture. She sent a message to Hirohito, half-hoping he wouldn't respond.

Sun respected the man as her mission superior, and could not help but to admire his beautiful yet deadly physical perfection, but too much time spent in his presence made her uncomfortable.

Hirohito was an alpha augment, and quite possibly the most valued clandestine operative in Asia Prime's Pacific division. Not only was his reputation impressive and fearsome in equal measure, but the level to which he had been upgraded with cyberware called into question, for Sun at least, the individual's basic humanity. He was what Sun imagined a god might be like, a being more human than human and yet almost entirely a machine.

She would have to undergo a debriefing on her attempted hack at some point today, and she knew he would have expected a notification as soon as she awoke. Much as she dreaded it, it was probably best to get it squared away. As soon as it was finished, she could get back to work. He had been there with her, on the operations deck, and certainly knew the process and outcomes of the day's activity. However, she had a feeling he wanted to know more about the Union slinger, as was his right, considering that when two legendary operators dueled it was a matter of significance.

All too soon, a message pinged in response, letting her know that Hirohito had agreed to meet with her and where to find him. There was barely enough time to slip on her shoes and shrug into her worn, favorite hoodie. She slung a mobile rig, waiting in a bag by the door, over her shoulder as she went. She never knew when she might be called to action. Sun, like most pro level slingers the world over, felt rather naked without a rig near to hand, and she wasn't about to engage Hirohito one on one lacking every psychological advantage she could muster.

Sun met him in his office, which rankled her a bit. Sun knew he had not chosen the destination to be inconsiderate. She was not sure her boss knew the meaning of the word, nor the implications, but it made her uneasy all the same. She would have felt more comfortable on her own turf, one of the many rooms used by slingers, her own private office, one of the dozen or so common areas scattered throughout the building. It was on the topmost floor (perhaps the entire topmost floor). Hirohito had a penchant for the extravagant, which was evident as soon as one stepped over the threshold and took in the lavish décor.

Sun didn't bother knocking. Hirohito was never surprised.

He was seated on the floor at a low small table, stirring a cup of tea, its twin sitting on the opposite side, in front of a small cushion. He tilted his head up slightly when he saw her, the corner of his mouth betraying his smile, before ducking it to take another measured sip. His hair, so light that there was no word for it but white, was styled perfectly, making her own hastily combed, short cut look shabby by comparison.

It was the same with nearly anything in Hirohito's company, it always came out second best. Despite her title as lead slinger of the operation, Sun would not have been shocked to learn that her boss could do just as well in the data-scape. He could certainly do everything else, that seemed what he'd been built for.

Hirohito was the head of the project in its entirety, their lead cyber agent, who coordinated and cleared nearly all of their operations involving or relating to the pulse of energy they hoped to harness. He held the leash of every slinger and engineer in the program. And that included Sun's, despite her high rank. The man was a living legend, even if most Prime operatives had not met him in person, which Sun felt was likely a good thing. He was so flawless, in body, manner, and skill, that he came off as something rather alien.

"Have you recovered?" he asked. The cadence of the words was wrong, curving down instead of up, though he still spoke them with false cheer. She had disappointed him. However close she had come to success, she had not done it. Not this time, at least.

Sun had not worked her way through the complex corporate culture of Asia Prime without learning the script. She smiled back, nodded twice, and sat down, setting her rig on the floor next to her before grabbing the cup of tea and taking her own careful drink. It was perfect, just the right amount of sugar and not too hot nor too close to cold. The art of tea was a delicate thing, requiring discipline and skill and was a cornerstone of their corporate culture. Sun could not help but to wonder if Hirohito had come by his tea prowess through measured training like most people, approaching it as a kind of meditation, or was he simply so augmented that his cyberware allowed him to bypass the traditional methods?

Her hollow stomach begged for more, and she had difficulty reigning in the urge to gulp it down. A platter of snacks appeared near the operatives after a few more quiet moments drinking tea together, placed there by a skinny looking man with the Asia Prime logo on his pressed shirt.

Apparently, Hirohito had commandeered one of the dining staff for his personal use. It didn't surprise her. The man had an almost pathological need for perfection, as any close observer could tell from his manner, the impeccable posture, and the careful way he shaped his words. The way he seemed to glide instead of walk, his footfalls nearly silent whatever the surface.

He let her clean half the platter, a light serving of fruit with yellow cakes and bean paste, before trying to start a proper conversation. In the meantime, she noted that he only ate half of one small apple, which he sliced with a knife rather than biting into it. He took each mouthful from where it was speared on the end of the blade, and she had the strange urge to see him miss and spear his lip or his tongue, to watch blood stain the pristine white suit he wore. Even his chewing seemed careful.

"He was better than I expected," she said at last when it became obvious that he meant for her to speak first. "Cole," she added. "I'd heard of him."

"We all have," Hirohito replied. "His file has now been disseminated to everyone on board, regardless of specialization. I made sure of it." He paused, tucking a single loose hair back into place. "It seemed a necessary precaution."

Sun nodded again, trying hard not to look too close at his face. The symmetry there was unnerving, and it was easy to drift too far in.

He was achingly attractive, so much so that she was certain he'd been upgraded with seduction augments. His gaze was a pitcher plant and it made her feel like an insect struggling in a trap. "I agree."

"If you agreed he was a threat, you should have taken him more seriously in the data-scape. The underestimation of him nearly cost Asia Prime your life." He speared another piece of fruit while he spoke, juice beading on the surface of the knife.

The words were not spoken with callous cruelty. They were spoken with little inflection at all, as were most of the things that Hirohito said. The lack of emotion had always disturbed her, but still more disturbing was the thought of seeing him truly incensed. She was glad, at least, not to have prompted that. Regardless of the lack of venom, the words still stung all the more because they were correct. She'd let her arrogance affect the hack; she simply hadn't expected as much fight out of Cole as she'd received, and by the time she realized how evenly matched they were, it was too late to rectify her poor choices. For all the perks of entering MassNet, the ability to reverse time while in its grip was not one. Or if it was, whoever had discovered it had kept the secret closely guarded.

"*Hai,*" she said simply, acknowledging his rightness with a slight bow of her head, "I will not fail again."

The smile he gave her suggested confidence in her abilities, reassurance, but because it was Hirohito, it did not touch his eyes, which she was positive weren't even real. "I am sending you files on a slinger known as Lunatic 8." He spoke the name with a tone that was the nearest to respect she'd ever heard from his lips. "When you return to operations, see what more you can uncover. Be cautious, this one should be considered a credible threat."

The rest of their talk had been practical, a more traditional debriefing, a recount of what she had done during the brief moments she had spent on the other side of Union Americana's firewalls. How best to approach the issue on their next attempt at breaching the wall of code. Every move, every decision she'd made during the hack and the ensuing battle had been picked apart, to the point that another headache, worse than the one she'd brought out of MassNet with her and worn all night. She staved it off with a second cup of tea the moment she'd left Hirohito's office for her own.

Sun wouldn't be able to avoid the man for long. Their jobs demanded that they work together, that they cooperate, and they did that much very well, but she could not bring herself to like him or be comfortable in his company. He would always seem too far removed from the rest of the world for friendship. The majority of slingers and cyber agents she had met were calculating; it was what the job demanded, but Hirohito was so cold as to seem nearly inhuman, and she could not imagine a future where the man's behavior did not put her on edge.

One of the advantages of having so few slingers on this mission was not having to explain her every action. Hirohito knew what she was up to, what her next course of action was, and that was all that mattered.

There was still work to be done.

Sun stared at the throne as though it was made of nails.

She needed to get herself back into the data-scape, to make some headway in learning more about the pulse and its location, the best way for their smaller, covert team to extract and harness its power. She and Hirohito had long ago formed the skeleton of a plan for when they zeroed in on the source of the energy, but depending upon she found (if she found anything) it would need some tweaking. Not to mention that when they began their plotting, they knew next to nothing about the Akiaten aside from rumors among the locals, picked up by the surveillance equipment they'd sent in in advance. That was before they'd even had any sightings.

Settling herself into the throne while still feeling the phantom aches from the previous stint was not her first choice, but her search would go faster in MassNet. That much she was sure of. She fitted the cables to their respective jack's blindly; after so many years, her fingers remembered the way without any input on her part. The throne was well made, and no one was permitted to use it save for her.

Asia Prime had spared no expense on fitting it to the contours of her body. The back of it curved against her spine, and the headpiece cradled her neck, keeping it from slanting into an awkward position during the hack.

In the early days of her career, before she'd picked up such generous benefactors, she'd often left CodeSource to find her chin resting on her shoulder and her neck stiff as hell where it had tilted toward one shoulder in consideration of some anomaly in the code. Her throne prevented any such incidents, holding her steady in its grip.

Sun rested her hands on opposite sides, letting them sink down into their rests, flexing her fingers. She entered the data-scape all at once, her mind switching from one plane to the next between blinks. It was not the gradual transition she had set out to make, and she immediately set about calming the panicked jolt that her breathing had turned to.

She saw the city again, mixed in with the constantly shifting code. She ran a sweep.exe, looking for anomalies in the code that might yield some trace of her quarry. The file on Lunatic 8 had indeed been slim, but it had indicated that the rogue slinger was something of a chaos factor. Sun had moved carefully into one of the regions Lunatic 8 was known to frequent, a part of the central city system. Her slinger cadre had been running sweeps, on Hirohito's order, for several hours, and Sun had used MassNet to appear as close to the target zone as she dared. This part of the scape was quiet, now, but the strings of code that made up the buildings and the street below her feet looked trampled upon, ravaged. Someone had ripped through this section of the data-scape, and from the sound of commotion somewhere ahead, they were still doing so. She code-chained a baffle.exe to obscure her presence and a shield.exe for protection before she turned toward the noise and followed the curious sounds.

It could only be Lunatic 8, the super-hacker that Hirohito had spoken of with such odd awe. Sun was still skeptical as she picked her way through the streets of code, eyes tracking the destruction she found along the way.

She recognized E-Bloc surveillance equipment, seen in the data-scape in their literal form, cameras of varying sizes, bugs configured to filter through the background noise of traffic and zoom in on voices, however quietly they whispered. Each one she passed was trashed, the imagined plastic backing melted or cracked, the screens blinking in distress. They'd each been fried from the inside out, and she had no doubt that the manifestation of the destruction in the real world was just as visible. There were likely a hundred techs at E-Bloc HQ struggling to keep their screens from going black.

When she was close enough to see, Sun was careful to keep absolutely silent, perfectly still. There would be no ripples in the code around her, nothing to give her away. The slinger she saw was on a rampage. A storm in the shape of a woman, smaller in stature than even Sun herself, her hair a tangled torrent of dull black around her head. Often, what one saw in the data-scape was not wholly true, someone might look fiercer or stronger, bulked up in armor, or made dangerous by a weapon hanging at their hip like the kill.exe Sun had automatically woven as a pistol the second her feet hit the coded ground.

This woman, Lunatic 8, looked lean and pale, but the words that first came to Sun's mind were skinny and gaunt, almost to the point of looking as though she suffered from some lingering sickness. Her eyes were sunken, but nonetheless bright, and burning with a deadly intelligence that Sun could see even from a distance. She took cover behind the corner of a building, shrouded in code, and settled in to watch.

Lunatic 8 hacked with the speed and precision of a whole slew of slingers, slashing and burning every bit of surveillance equipment her coding could reach, before moving on to the next sector and doing the same. Her movements had the same unnerving fluidity that the rest of the Akiaten boasted, though Sun had trouble picturing her doing the rest of the acrobatic routine. The slinger was a hurricane of attack programs. The force of the slashing was so much that it reverberated off their surroundings, sending vibrations through the air. Sun felt it in her cables, an uncomfortable shift. She paused to strengthen the shield she'd placed around herself, hoping the strength of the slinger's attacks would not fry her own equipment by extension. Sun was intrigued. She wasn't done watching just yet.

She knew what perfect hacking looked like, and Lunatic 8's movements were damn near that. For all the might and skill that the likes of Hayden Cole and herself were capable of, this rampaging being was on an entirely different level. There was no way to record what you saw in the data-scape, seeing as each person's brain interpreted the sights as they saw fit, but Sun found herself wishing that she could. There was no way she could explain this with the proper words, and as a slinger, words were not her strong suit anyway.

Hirohito had told her little about Lunatic 8, and she knew that he knew little himself. Their sources only told them that she was a slinger for the Akiaten. There was little mention of her skill or what experience had made her so formidable. Sun watched the code sluice between Lunatic 8's fingers, her face twisting into a snarl as she demolished yet another section of E-Bloc tech, sending E-Bloc slingers retreating into alleys and doorways, while yet others jerked and twisted as what appeared to Sun as lighting from the woman's fingers fried them where they stood. There would be dying slingers in the E-Bloc HQ, of that Sun was certain. The Akiaten slinger looked a second away from imploding, the heat of her attacks turning inward, and Sun was positive that somewhere out there Lunatic 8 was pushing so much data and energy that her own surge protectors were probably melting.

Sun watched until there was nothing else to learn. There was no reason to intervene, aside from not being back to her full strength, it would only be detrimental to stop the woman from destroying the E-Bloc surveillance. Lunatic 8 had not set out to help Asia Prime in any way, of that Sun was sure, but it was moving them ahead in the game all the same. The woman was doing the same for Americana, however indirectly.

In Sun's opinion, it was Americana who were the real threat to Asia Prime's slinging operations. E-Bloc had superior troops to all of them, but they were nothing if no one could confirm the location of the pulse. She would prefer eliminating the inconvenience of E-Bloc's ground operation, and this put them one step closer to that goal. She wondered if Hirohito had known what the Akiaten was up to in MassNet if in telling her to remain an observer, he was condoning her inaction. It would take E-Bloc's team of slingers, those who survived the attack, ages to recover.

She watched until Lunatic 8 faded from the code, and then emerged herself. This time, no pain accompanied the exit, and none of her equipment was half-melted or dying. She double-checked the notes of Lunatic 8 she'd taken while in the 'scape and sent them Hirohito. His heads-up display was never off, and she knew he'd get them immediately, whatever he might be up to. Sun powered down the systems enmeshed with the throne and unhooked herself from the cables still in her neck.

Sliding slowly from the seat, she gave the throne a parting pat, and tucked a few dangling wires back into place. The time on her display told her she'd been gone for more than hour, but less than two. It had felt longer inside; the code was curious that way, bending and shifting in ways you never expected it to.

Sometime later, she circled her office. It was smaller than Hirohito's, small enough to pace without losing breath. The tea she'd been sipping before entering MassNet had long since gone cold, steam fading into nothing. She poured the contents down the sink and went in search of another to drink while she started a file on Lunatic 8. They would need more to fill it, and she was up to the task. Sun had brushed up against something wild, untamed, and impossibly destructive. She was as fascinated as she was intimidated.

Hirohito read through the file. He knew that it was only the first of many. Now that Sun's curiosity had been ignited, he would be hard pressed to keep her out of MassNet long enough to accomplish anything else they needed. Lunatic 8 was, as yet, an unknown factor (and he hated unknowns). They knew she held a respected position among the Akiaten's resistance group, that she was a slinger of some sort, and that her name was whispered like a legend. But before he'd sent Sun in, he'd known little else.

Find her, he sent back. Continue to observe. But do not engage.

Even such a simple request was likely to be no easy task. So far, nothing had been easy when it came to the Akiaten. He needed more. And it would go faster with two of them looking. Still wearing his immaculate white suit, Hirohito stepped carefully into the tailored outer layer of material that hugged his form and fell all the way to his feet, melding into boots of the same make. It was high-end fabric, the best that Asia Prime's nearly unlimited funding could buy. Called a shimmer suit, it refracted the light around it to the point that the wearer became next to invisible. It was the sort of thing you would only notice if you were looking for it, and unlike the cloaking technology used by the higher tech soldiers, its effectiveness did not waver with movement or a drastic change of scenery.

He pulled up his HUD with the blink of an eye, using it to mark the coordinates of the location of the E-Bloc firefight a few days past. The scene would have already been picked over by now, but he might well find something that had been missed by the other corporations. Or perhaps, by now, the Akiaten themselves had circled back and left new evidence.

8

Hayden still felt close to dead when he woke. He would have liked to spend a few more hours recuperating, he could still research and even run CodeSource from the comfort of his couch, but his day was jump-started when he received a message from Mitchell calling for the team to meet in one of the smaller conference rooms within the next half hour. His stomach felt shot through and sour, so he eased his way into eating a nutrient bar with a cup of subpar coffee made from the outdated pot on the room's counter. He wasn't sure if the real issue was himself or the pot, but the coffee was more hot water than flavor and he screwed up his face as he sipped it. It took a few more sips for the fog to clear and for him to remember that the off-kilter sense of taste was one of the side effects of the equilibrium pills.

Companies the world over had worked on reducing the side effects, which was good. Hayden could remember his first days as a teen slinger and how the pills would irritate his bowels and worsen his acne. If bland tasting coffee was the worst of it, that seemed like a fair deal, even if the disappointment kind of set the mood for the morning.

He wasn't sure if he felt up to the casual conversations that might ensue if he took himself to the dining facility, and instead walked to the indicated meeting room and sat with his coffee warming his hands as he waited for the others to arrive. It might be sweltering outside the compound, but there was enough high-end hardware indoors that the temperature was kept at the low end, partly for the sake of the equipment and partly to help mask their presence from any satellite sweeps that might pass overhead.

Mitchell arrived just as Hayden found a mildly comfortable position in a chair that was no doubt made to be uncomfortable.

Mitchell's face was drawn tight with worry, a sight that Hayden found rather disconcerting. Captain Mitchell might be a hard case when it came to protocol, but he was one of the most experienced non-augment operators Hayden had ever met. If a man who could walk through third world war zones was rattled, this morning was going to get worse than bad coffee.

Hayden wondered, as he had since he dragged himself from bed, what he had missed during his convalescence. The Captain fiddled with one of the ports near the empty wall at the front of the room, the sort that allowed holograms to transmit. Hayden half stood to help him with it, being quicker with any sort of technology than most people (and almost definitely quicker than those he classed as soldiers), but Mitchell waved off the help and he allowed himself to sink back down.

"If I couldn't manage to set it up," Mitchell said wryly, "I wouldn't be in charge of anything."

Hayden smirked in response and thought that perhaps Mitchell could have used the chance to crash for eighteen hours as well. Guys like him always pushed themselves right up to the edge of collapse, must be a military thing.

"Sorry, Cap," he said, keeping his voice even, knowing how easy it was to mistake sarcastic teasing for outright hostility when one had gone too long with their brain in overdrive. Mitchell was stressed, there was no denying that, otherwise, such an organized, by-the-book man would not have called a mandatory meeting out of the blue.

"Basilica's written up another speech then?" Hayden asked, trying to lighten the mood.

"The man certainly missed his calling as a politician," Mitchell answered, the tension in his shoulders lessening ever so slightly, plugging the last cord to the port and standing when the Union Americana logo slotted into place, "But yes, there have been a number of developments and he wants to spin things."

The Captain sat down in his usual spot at one end of the table, drummed his knuckles on the hard plastic, checked the time half a dozen times in the space of two minutes. There had been a half hour window before the time of the meeting, and Hayden had started downstairs almost as soon as he read it, hoping to be more alert and awake by the time they got around to actual business.

"You mind giving me a run-down?" he asked gingerly before sipping his now lukewarm coffee, "I haven't had a chance to touch base with anyone since I got out of MassNet."

Mitchell's already stressed face contorted further as he pulled activated his ocular HUD, the one bit of cyberware augmentation that was a universal upgrade for all Union field staff, searching through what Hayden could only imagine were his sent files. The things that had been pulled up and skimmed through recently enough to be relevant.

"I thought I had," Mitchell said, as close to an apology as Hayden thought the man could get. He nodded his understanding, then settled in. as Mitchell gave him what he assured Hayden was a vastly abridged version of the past day.

"We didn't so much as send Laine out, as she just decided to go. You know how it works with her, as does Basilica. He assures me that this problem with protocol that the two of you seem to share gets results, regardless of my reservations," Mitchell began. "Only just got her report in around the middle of last night. Haven't read through it as thoroughly as I would like, but I'll send you a copy right now. There's no sense in you having no clue what we're talking about." Mitchell looked around the empty room with a tired frown. "That is if anyone else plans on showing up without having to be escorted."

Hayden tried for a smile. Hoped it didn't look as fabricated as it felt. "Don't get ahead of yourself boss. We've still got a good half hour before Bascilica graces us with his digital presence."

Mitchell snorted but seemed too tired for the usual comeback he would have been up for.

"Near as I can tell, Laine followed those local assholes who sprung the attack on the E-Bloc soldiers to a safe-house out on the edge of the city, where the jungle is starting to reclaim the sprawl. She thought there might be something worth looking at inside, but it appeared to be have been hollowed out and shuttered not long before she got there, which is what the intel analysists gathered from her pictures as well.

"She was in the middle of investigating what was left behind by the Akiaten, organic samples and a few homemade gamma loads when a squad of E-Bloc soldiers zeroed in on the house. Laine dispatched the soldiers," he continued, with a pointed looked at Hayden, as if to say who would expect anything else. "It's her assessment that the entire encounter was set up by the Akiaten, in hopes of getting rid of either our agents or the E-Bloc soldiers." Mitchell shrugged, then continued.

"Or, they may have just wanted to see who each side would send. How we would respond to a threat in an unfamiliar environment. Regardless of the motive, Laine got played, and while she might have struck a blow to E-Bloc, we've tipped our hand and now everyone knows we have an alpha augment in play."

Hayden tried to keep his face more or less blank, still working through the explanation. It didn't surprise him that Laine had struck out on her own, no less than it had surprised Mitchell. The corporation certainly wouldn't condone such tactics in an official capacity, but Hayden already knew that no one would be reprimanding Laine for it.

However bad such things looked to the higher ups, he had no illusions that they didn't realize how necessary such decisions sometimes were. Every organization worth its salt had a few effective loose cannons. Laine was theirs, as loyal as she was unpredictable, almost to a fault. He was grateful when Mitchell didn't immediately start trying to draw his opinion out. It gave him time to assess the files the captain had uploaded and sent along as he'd been speaking.

Hayden pulled his heads-up display to the forefront of his vision and dug through the files. There was one from Nibiru that he filed away for later, and a few on his personal account that he made a point of not checking except through his personal terminal and in private, it was too easy to slice the wireless that the HUDs operated off of when in HQ. Laine's report seemed to have been run through by their security teams since she submitted it, as there were footnotes and underlined sections throughout. A few lines trailed into the margins with coordinates noted along the sides. It was far more complex than the shortened version given to him by Mitchell; the terminology scattered throughout was closer to professional, sprinkled with explanations that were on par with military briefings.

Everything Mitchell had told him seemed to be in order, but Hayden found himself wrapped up in Laine's wording in a way that he hadn't quite been in Mitchell's. He could picture her killing each soldier she mentioned, blood on the leaves, each grisly detail. It was like a poet's recollection of carnage, and though he'd read other such reports by Laine, the sickening artistry of it always engaged and repulsed him at the same time.

He was still skimming through the last lines when Nibiru walked inside, dropping down beside of him with a guilty look at her watch. Her eyes darted from him to Mitchell.

"So, I'm not late?"

"We're early," Hayden said. "Thought I might need a minute to catch up. You read Laine's report yet?"

She nodded. "Last night. Crazy huh? The Akiaten laying out a trap like that."

"We haven't confirmed that it was a trap," Mitchell began.

"I say it was a trap." Laine was quick to cut him off. She stood just by the open door, having entered in virtual silence. She closed it with a quiet click as she spoke, her voice making Nibiru jump and Hayden tense. She gave Mitchell her sharp, not-quite-successful smile, which in Hayden's mind made it all the more terrifying. Sometimes she really did come off more like a machine than a person. "Is that not good enough for you?"

Captain Mitchell wasn't the type to be shaken by anyone, and the captain was too familiar with the uncanny mannerisms of alpha augments to fall prey to the intimidation. "It doesn't matter if it's good enough for me." He jerked his head toward the rotating logo, reached out to run a finger through the immaterial hologram. "It has to be good enough for them."

Silence did not reign long before Nibiru broke it, either uncaring of the tense atmosphere or not familiar enough with the team to read it accurately, as she cut through the quiet with her usual, easy conversation.

"I never got a buzz that I'd been promoted, so I'm assuming you're brain damage free," she said to Hayden in a pleasantly casual tone, tacking a question on to the end of the statement.

Hayden rubbed a hand over his face, realizing that he must have still looked vaguely like shit for her to be asking such a question.

"I hope so," he answered simply. "I'm not drooling or seeing spots and the med staff haven't told me otherwise... yet."

She grinned, eyes moving absently across her display as she waited. "Don't worry about your slingers," she said. "Overdog is surprisingly competent for being so outdated, he might not have the upgrades to ride the tech but he's good at running the crew. And no one's tried to break in since you've been out for the count." She lowered her voice conspiratorially. "Wasted opportunity if you ask me. I understand E-Block leaving us be, they wouldn't have known you were out of commission unless they'd been watching, but it would have been the best time for Asia Prime to sweep in."

Laine's interest was piqued. "Perhaps they have fewer slingers on their roster than we thought," she said.

"Maybe," Hayden said. "Or they've got too much on their plate to be picking more fights, same as we do. The Akiaten could be giving them trouble."

Laine nodded. "There's no reason to assume they would concentrate their efforts on us. They've hit E-Bloc, and us, but as far as we're aware, they haven't gone for Prime. It's odd, don't you think?"

Hayden was still considering his answer when the logo winked out, replaced rapidly by Bascilica. The display was close to him, and he was visible only from mid-torso up, like some ridiculous, detailed bust. The suit he wore looked even nicer than the one he'd graced them with last time, and Hayden paused a moment to wonder exactly how much of their budget went to the man's wardrobe.

Though Hayden hadn't seen him in person more than a couple of times, he was confident that he had never once seen the man in the same piece of clothing. Everything, down to his socks and his sunglasses, seemed to be exchanged by the next meeting, even if it fell on the same day.

Bascilica looked distinctly unimpressed as his eyes flitted about the small room, as though he'd been expecting something more. Perhaps, Hayden thought, the four of them simply didn't look glad enough to see him. They'd have to schedule another meeting right after and give everyone time to perfect their bullshitting faces.

Laine, oddly, looked closer to passing this unspoken test than the rest of them. She at least looked interested in the proceedings, and raised her brows in anticipation, waiting for what Bascilica would decree, probably crossing her fingers that an order for an assault or an assassination was on the way.

Mitchell still looked a mix of exhausted, and like he'd greatly enjoy the chance to shoot something. That may have been why he and Laine never needled each other too badly. However much she strayed from protocol, they could at least bond over the feeling of a pulled trigger and the often-messy aftermath.

Nibiru's face, by contrast, was turned toward Hayden, one eyebrow raised, lip quirking side-ways. He glanced discreetly at his display as a new message appeared.

Look who decided to show up, it read.

He only hoped Bascilica thought the slight snort that escaped him was due to something other than idle shit-talking aimed at his boss.

He kicked Nibiru lightly under the table and was relieved when she caught on and turned her gaze to Bascilica, who was pretending not to be concerned with the state of his team and almost immediately launched into a discussion of both Hayden's work in MassNet, and Laine's reconnaissance mission turned gunfight. He spoke with his usual enthusiasm, gesturing hugely with his arms. Hayden suspected he was stepping from side to side as he spoke as well. It was a tick of the man's that he noticed before, and the hologram skipped every few moments as it struggled to track his movements.

He had little to say about Hayden's encounter with Sun in MassNet, though he was quick to commend him for his work, and even quicker to remind him just how much of a threat Sun and her team were.

"I'll have you and the rest of our slingers here work on uncovering her location. It's at least as important as finding out where these Akiaten are primarily based." Bascilica's hands moved off-screen, giving the brief illusion that his arms end at the elbow. He moved them back shortly, but Hayden could tell he was looking at something in his own space, far away from Manila.

"Despite our best efforts, our analysts have been unable to suss out much more regarding the Akiaten, even with the additional footage and data secured by you and your people on the ground. Our only new information comes from the attack on E-Bloc witness by Cole and the information Laine and our security forces gathered from the scene of the attack. It isn't much, but based on their tactical patterns, the working theory is that they have at least one or more slingers aiding their resistance efforts.

Overdog has confirmed that someone hit a number of the E-Bloc field installations through MassNet. They picked up on the fallout through CodeSource, though we don't have a firm grasp of how much of

E-Bloc's digital infrastructure was damaged and to what extent. Suffice it to say, these locals aren't just farmers with pistols. E-Bloc is hurting, and after Cole's duel with Sun, the Prime front has been quiet, but that doesn't help us find these Akiaten unless we can come across them in the data-scape or they decide to make an obvious move against us physically or digitally."

He paused, looked rather hard at Nibiru who was still toying with her heads-up display. Hayden had no doubt that she was working on something remotely, though he didn't know what, but he found Bascilica's assumption that she wasn't paying attention rather amusing and had to fight off a rising smile. He was quite sure it would help Bascilica's opinion if he kept his face blank and professional, so that was what he did, though not before nudging Nibiru with his foot once more.

Mitchell, arms crossed, still sitting up straight in his chair. "So much for our standard resource extraction."

Hayden failed in his mission keep his face blank, and Nibiru chuckled.

Bascilica spoke quickly in an attempt to keep the meeting, to keep his speech, flowing along smoothly according to the bullets on the outline he was no doubt peeking at out of their view. "Regardless of their combat prowess and unknown slinger cadre, the brick wall we're experiencing with the locals is a standard defiance pattern. It's nothing we haven't seen before, especially you, Captain, with that business in Belgrade, and certainly nothing to grow overly concerned about.

"Between our security teams and our slinging—er, hacking, slicing, whatever the slang, teams, I'm sure we'll learn more in no time and have this place pacified." The smile he wore was much too wide to be real and looked stuck to his face, as though someone had sewn it there and left the stitches to fester.

He was just as worried as the rest of them. Maybe more, Hayden thought.

"This is just," Bascilica spread his hands, "Something that happens in these low-grade regions. Unlike the rest of us, they have yet to reap any benefits from the postwar surge. This is known."

Had Hayden been less familiar with his methods, he might have been taken in by the wording and the confidence.

"We cannot deny, however, that this makes our job more difficult. That's why we're prepared to back up any actions that this team deems necessary to accomplish the mission. We have the local government well in hand, so it shouldn't be too complicated to persuade them to look the other way, as kowtowed as they are with E-Bloc." Bascilica forced a laugh. "E-Bloc has a strong presence, they've all but declared martial law. From what our sources tell us, there won't be anyone positioned to get in the way of a small, high-end team." He swept his eyes over the four of them, giving each of them an assessing look that lingered too long to be comfortable. "That's where each of you come in."

There were a few more boisterous sentences pumped full of misplaced confidence before Bascilica gave them all one more salesman's grin, and the holograph winked out sight, faltering for a moment before the logo slotted back into place. All of them stared at the space where their boss no longer stood for a long moment before Nibiru, characteristically, broke the strained silence.

"Did that sound like a steaming pile of shit to anyone else, or is it just me?"

"Just you," Hayden tried to joke, still too tired to think of anything clever, and the engineer rolled her eyes. He looked to Mitchell and the slinger shook his head to showcase his displeasure.

"Union Americana is good at extracting value from low-grade regions, regardless of how hard the locals push back, but this is not as standard as he's pretending it is. I've seen the Akiaten in action, and you have all seen the footage. These resistance guys move and fight like alpha augments, and not just one or two, but all of them."

Nibiru shrugged. "Wouldn't be surprised. I agree though, those guys are supremely badass. I'm half convinced they have as many brains on their payroll as we do. We can't expect to just shoot our way out of this, that strategy doesn't seem to be working out so well for E-Bloc."

"We'll have to engage them asymmetrically," Laine agreed, looking unabashedly pleased with the thought. As nervous as Hayden was about the prospect, he felt a stir of excitement in his own veins as well. As dangerous as his fight with Sun had been, it had been the biggest challenge he'd faced against a slinger in years and he had the distinct impression that the Akiaten were going to prove themselves equally impressive in the physical realm.

"If they're as organized as you think, Laine, they'd have to have their own slingers," Hayden said. "Hell, I wouldn't be surprised if they're keeping closer tabs on us than we are on them."

Mitchell stood, swiped a hand angrily through the rotating logo, and began to pace the length of the small room.

"Fighting insurgents is never easy, especially when we know for a fact the locals are covering for them where they can. This is gonna turn into a quagmire real fucking quick if we don't put together a plan that's more complex than: 'They'll be too busy to notice'. That goes for E-Bloc and Asia Prime as well. Cole's right. They might already have our movements zeroed." He put a hand on the back of his neck, fingers grasping at the short, steel gray hair that covered his scalp. He shook his head as though to shake loose Bascilica's clinging words. "Calling it a standard defiance pattern is just a way of belittling the issue. Easy for a suit to say."

Laine met the Captain eyes. "Not so easy for a grunt?"

"Exactly," he agreed, and Hayden marveled again at the strange understanding between the two.

Dressed in her armor as always, Laine tapped the nail of her index finger against the flexible outer layer that covered her knee, twisted her face into a thoughtful expression. She looked to Hayden, hoping their thoughts tended the same way, as they often did when it came to their hope of a challenge.

"At least it will be fun," she said.

Hayden nodded once in passive agreement, but internally, his insides were churning. He loved a good fight in the data-scape, but Bascilica was talking about gambling with more than one life, against an enemy they still knew next to nothing about. Obviously considering the meeting over and done with, as eager to work as he'd ever seen her, Laine stood and vacated the room with a hollow, parting smile.

Nibiru's body language had remained relaxed throughout, leaning back in her chair, tilting forward with her hands splayed on the tabletop to hold her weight. Her voice though held an edge of worry, or perhaps resentment at the casual way Bascilica had referred to the battles they faced.

"This is how it always seems to go. Places like this—the ones that they have resources everyone's so ready to kill for—they're always the ones that never got anything out of the war, to begin with."

She pushed a lock of her hair back from her forehead and sighed.

Nibiru is right, Hayden thought, listening to Laine's boots echo down the hall and realizing that the operative wanted everyone to hear her as if her footfalls were the beat of war drums. She'd left the door open, obviously expecting the rest of them to leave shortly. After all, she must be thinking, what was there left to talk about.

He knew what Nibiru meant, and could tell from the look on Mitchell's face that he knew it, too. Most of the world, Union Americana included, came out of the war better off, faster, richer, healthier, and with more combined resources than they'd begun with, but the places that were already third world hellholes had stayed that way. It had always been a tough thing for Hayden to accept, but keeping a good chunk of the population desperate made them easier to dominate, to exploit.

Unlike the guilt that was stirring in Hayden's chest, Mitchell simply looked accepting. The Captain may not have liked the way Bascilica was doing things, but it was plain on his face that he believed a sacrifice of some sort necessary. He was prepared for casualties, for collateral damage, as if the transition from war for oil to war for energy was as smooth as changing the name of the balance sheet. He nodded at Nibiru's words, but what he answered with wasn't what any of them wanted to hear, except perhaps, for the already absent Laine.

"Somebody's always got to lose." Captain Mitchell stated.

Nibiru huffed an angry breath through her nose but said nothing else. She slung her rig over her shoulder with a frustration that sent it swinging from side to side as she left the room. She cast a hopeful glance at Hayden over her shoulder, but he was still too stunned to follow. Her feet, despite being lighter, echoed louder than Laine's in the hallway as she stormed down the hallway.

He wanted to argue with Mitchell himself. As irritated as the man had looked at the way Bascilica had handled things, it shouldn't take much convincing, but the longer he hesitated, the more determined the Captain looked. Hayden watched him gather his things, turn off the hologram, then head to the door at his back. Hayden rose and followed him. His feelings must have shown clearly enough on his face because before he and Mitchell parted ways in the hallway, the captain turned to him.

"I wasn't lying," he said.

Hayden wanted to feel angry, but he was only, oddly, very tired, despite the sleep of the past day.

"I know, Captain," he said. "You don't do it half as well as Bascilica. I've seen you try."

Mitchell nodded once, his smile halfway there. He appreciated Hayden's attempt at lightheartedness but recognized how feigned it was. Perhaps they had worked together long enough to find their rhythm, him and Mitchell, and Laine. They knew each other's strengths, fears, facial expressions. On more than one occasion, their lives would no doubt depend on such nuances.

"I've got kids to keep fed," Mitchell said simply. "This is good money, and if it wasn't us doing this dirty job it would be somebody else." He looked rather hard at Hayden as he said this, as though he needed the reminder. "If things get harder, just remember that."

It was good advice. Hayden watched his back disappear around the corner. He had joined for the money, the rare sense of security that came for a slinger with steady work, it was a rare thing, and he recognized, even in the beginning, how lucky he'd been to score a job of such caliber. He was in it for the challenge too, much as it disquieted him to share the same ambition as Laine. Bascilica's words did not negate either of these criteria. Hayden should have been happy with the gig he had, and he was, mostly. He just couldn't shake the feeling of guilt, of responsibility, when Bascilica spoke as he did.

It was a hard thing to think on. Hayden took his now cold, watery coffee to his workspace at the opposite end of the lower level, noting the conspicuous absence of Nibiru from the space across from him, and dove into his work. There were a thousand things that might have gone awry in his absence, and each one required confirmation of its continued functionality before he even considered doing anything else. He needed to speak with Overdog, hear his report on what the team of slingers had been up to while he was out of commission. He needed to think about what he was paid to think about, and nothing more.

Fuck it, he thought, this island nation was going to get exploited one way or the other. The philosophy and the responsibility were someone else's problem, someone who didn't have bills to pay. He had a job to do and a paycheck to collect. We're all mercs here, and we know it.

9

Nibiru had been hard at work. Hayden had never disputed that fact that she was dedicated, but he hadn't expected the level of skill so apparent in a project she'd completed so quickly.

Americana had several sets of drones at their disposal, but these were the first they had been issued, to Hayden's knowledge, that were virtually undetectable.

They were called dragonfly drones for a reason and looked nearly exactly like their namesakes, made from a light shimmering metal equipped with tiny microphones, cameras, and all-purpose sensors. They flew in swarms, spreading our or bunching together in groups as the occasion merited, each of them transmitting the gathered data to the others so that if one or many were lost, the information would still have a chance of making it back to their security team and analysts.

Nibiru would manage them herself and could do so easily enough as long as she was jacked into the system, using the HQ's native CodeSource network to direct the swarm and manage their various directions. From her work station, while in the coding trance of the system, Nibiru could multitask to such a degree that she could accomplish solo what would take ten traditional pilots to match.

"We have to custom assemble these things in the field, to ensure that they are perfectly calibrated to the operating environment. No pre-packaged short cuts. What do you think?" she asked, slightly out of breath from the explanation, her voice holding an undertone of nervousness, as if she half expected him to shoot her down, even staring at the finished product in front of them, where he hunched over to give it a closer look.

It felt fragile under his large hands, and he almost feared he would break it when he caught one of the wings between two fingers and tested the feel.

"I think," he said, looking up from the desk to find her anxious gaze. "That you might have just saved our asses."

Her face dropped into a relieved grin. "Awesome. These are about as experimental as it gets, but I'm feeling good about it, they're going to be analyzing what we do here for years. The only thing to fret about now is that they can still be hacked while they're deployed." She gave him a hopeful look. "But I was hoping you'd have some advice on that."

He thought about making a show of hesitating, but he decided that today he wasn't that cruel. "I can do better than advice."

It was only a matter of clearing the plan with Mitchell, who was happy enough to hear about more possible intelligence.

Hayden had no doubt they would stumble upon something that would be useful. Nibiru would be in CodeSource, jacked in to control each nuance of movement exhibited by the dragonfly drones. Hayden would be in MassNet, fighting off any attacks from the rival corporations, in addition to doing what he could to keep the drones below radar. They could run simulations all day, but a field test in actual operational conditions was the only way to smooth the edges of this new tech, not to mention further solidify Hayden and Nibiru's ability to work in tandem across both digital realms.

She set up shop at a desk he'd dragged into the throne room, the close proximity allowing them to link their displays so that could track each other's progress in addition to the drones. Hayden sat, tried to force his body to relax despite it well remembering the stress he'd placed it under the last time he sat there. He plugged in his jack, gave Nibiru a nod, and watched her do the same before his vision faded out.

Any reservations he had about getting back into the throne were gone as the datascape rushed to greet his senses as if welcoming him home.

He could see her movements in the code as soon as he slotted in, able to pick out the patterns and associate them with the engineer. His imagination presented him with an ethereal cityscape, covered in layer upon layer of snaking cables that pulsed with energy and purpose.

He found his metaphor for Nibiru once he recognized the cascading patterns of her moving through CodeSource, and he found himself wondering what she might look like to him if she too were jacked into MassNet. People who created code as they went moved differently through the strands of energy. When the abstract energy pattern that was Nibiru activated the drone swarm, Hayden witnessed her presence arc out of the cables and emerge onto the digital streets.

Rather than simply riding the cables, following the prescribed movements as Hayden might have in her place, Nibiru went where she chose to, winding her way through data in looping, intricate paths. And where there were no paths, no viable directions, she simply steeled herself and made new ones.

The drones, which of course looked just like dragonflies in Hayden's metaphor, moved just as easily as their creator. It was like watching a cloud of shimmering insects coalesce to form a humanoid shape that was their master, and then disperse again as they sped off in a multitude of directions.

Hayden could not fit moving parts together and make them run, could not bring things to life outside of MassNet, yet Nibiru had given them this after a scant few days of work. Granted, they could have used a bit more time to test them, a few days devoted to test runs. Extra time, in this case though, was hard to come by. Hayden wouldn't have been shocked to learn that she always worked like this, as though she was under a deadline before she'd even been given one.

Nibiru might be younger than Hayden, but she was smart enough to understand that her profession was often undersold. No one truly understood how much work went into engineering unless they had a rudimentary understanding of the work, and it was very seldom that people went out of their way to learn. She had discovered a long time ago that bit of advance planning on her part went a long way. She was going to go far with the Union, of that Hayden was becoming most certain.

The manifestations of the swarm within the code looked as shimmering and beautiful as they did in the real world. He imagined them flying low over streets and rooftops, skirting their way through alleys and under cars, coming out unscathed on the other side.

His visualization of the city came to life around him as he worked, buildings rising up from the black, blank surface below him, streets stretching out, the details gradually filling in. Far away, he could see the code rippling still more, and he knew that Nibiru had followed her plan and used a good half of the drones to glide into the rural, forested areas that lay in the same direction in which Laine had found the safe house.

This run was more about establishing an environmental baseline, a rough map of sorts from which they could hone their search and monitor their own progress, not to mention keep the likes of Bascilica well plied with updates.

From there, they spread out further. Hayden saw them both as irregularities in the code and as glinting insects in the sky. First sticking together in tight bands and packs, but then drifting apart as if carried by the wind, until it was a challenge for even Hayden to keep track of them all. Thankfully, the network connected the drones. If one of them was compromised, the others relayed the message across the system. For now, though, there were no alerts.

The dragonfly drones continued on their set courses, veering one way or another only when Nibiru adjusted their routes. Some of them left his line of vision only to flit back in, the code shifting to accommodate them.

Hayden felt as if he was watching an entirely new professional specialization being pioneered right in front of him as Nibiru displayed a slinger's level of cognitive fluidity, using the jack to compartmentalize her mind in order to pilot each individual drone and yet simultaneously existing as the master of the entire swarm.

It felt good to finally get proactive about locating the energy source. So much of their day to day since arriving had been focused on the deadly dance of move and countermove against the operatives of Asia Prime and E-Bloc. That was generally how protracted field missions like this unfolded. The competing operations skirmished with each other in both analog and digital confrontations, testing each other as they jockeyed for position. The trick of being successful in such situations was for the field managers to masterfully toggle between the escalating conflict against competitors and actually doing the job they'd been sent to do.

In this case, finally getting the drones in the air and establishing a search parameter felt good, and Hayden could sense that in everyone's mood. With so little to go on about the energy source, beyond Bascilica and the Union's insistence of fortunes to be won in the acquisition of this new power, the team was ready to get to work on something meaningful. First, they had to zero in on a reliable way of tracking the energy in a microcosm. Presently the best that the Union satellites could give them was the island nation itself, anything more focused was for the team on the ground to pioneer and then track it back to its source, as all such emanations had a nexus point.

It would have been easy to get caught up in the way that Nibiru worked, and for a moment, he almost forgot that he was not there solely as an observer. He worked to keep all his senses focused on spotting possible threats, but it was still more luck than anything when he spotted the code began to light up around them as they drew attention.

Most of the dragonflies, as expected, remained under the radar without arousing suspicion, but a few, a handful, but a handful were enough, must have registered as anomalies, not quite matching the flight pattern of an actual insect or else flying over spots equipped with sensors that would register the unfamiliar hardware. It appeared that some scraps of the E-Bloc security grid had survived the Akiaten slinger's rampage. He'd known that this was a probable issue, though honestly, he'd hoped they would be able to lens more ground before hostile flares went up.

The ensuing response looked like a fireworks show inside MassNet. The strings of data started blinking and shifting as they were assaulted by slingers jacking in and opening up as soon as they came online.

Hayden recognized the organized, sector by sector cones of fire that identified the slingers as E-Bloc. They had the discipline of a military outfit, even in the data-scape, and Hayden found himself wondering if they recruited slingers from among their own soldiers. The E-Bloc slingers were hurling attack programs in all directions, and Hayden's imagination translated that into what appeared to be a lattice work of anti-air tracer fire rising from several places in the cityscape. It reminded him of footage he'd see of night bombing raids during the first and second oil wars of the Middle East, where gunners who did not have any clue where the enemy was fired wildly into the air, knowing only that they were indeed under attack.

Taking care to keep himself and the ripples of his actions hidden, Hayden frowned in concentration as he hid the drones that he could, generating spherical shielding around the flares that surfaced in the code each time the drone's onboard software recorded something their programming found worthy.

Most of the dragonflies managed to escape attention, either because they were already almost out of range, or because of his ongoing damage control. The enemy certainly knew that there were surveillance drones in play, even if they did not realize the specifics. A few of them may have been spotted, but that didn't mean E-Bloc had a clear idea of just how many drones there actually were. If he could keep their attention focused on just a few, Nibiru could make the others move on with the plan.

He hoped she caught on to his movements through the link in their systems and understood just what he was getting at. He dared not broadcast to her now that there were hostiles searching the datascape for them, which was terribly strange considering that their bodies were right next to each other. Even if she didn't quite grasp his tactics, Hayden had faith enough in her ability to improvise that he wasn't too worried.

Until he spotted Sun's entrance to the data-scape.

Both she and E-Bloc were scanning for rogue signals, like kicking a hornet's nest to unleash a horde of angry attackers, and though Sun's tech was more advanced, they were both closing in on spotting more and more of the drones, pinging their positions and locking on. A few more seconds and the dragonflies would be zeroed and under direct assault.

Shit, Hayden thought.

He knew better than to assume that Asia Prime and E-Bloc had banded together. It would take true desperation to bring them to that, and however difficult this mission had been so far, it didn't warrant that level of compromise between such steadfast enemies.

As he tried to shield Nibiru and her drones from the notice of the E-Bloc slingers, Hayden noticed that their movements seemed unusually difficult to track and dodge as though they were aware that he was fighting off the two of them at once and had adapted to coordinate their attacks.

He noticed a nearby building shift as if the dimensions of the architecture had been altered, and what had been a sharp curve in the street below became a wide avenue. E-Bloc hackers moved through it, seemingly unaware of the change in the environment, and that's when it hit him.

Someone was playing with the foundations of the MassNet landscape!

Out there in the code, somewhere, was a slinger making it easier for the enemy. At first, he was incredulous at the thought that the Akiaten hacker was behind it. Why would someone powerful enough for such devastation earlier pit the competitors against each other?

Then he realized it was all about the drones.

Whoever it was out there, was feeding the E-Bloc security grid with data on the drones, but doing it in such a way that either the E-bloc cadre didn't realize it wasn't coming from them or didn't care. Now he understood why some of their grid survived, that Akiaten slinger had intentionally left enough of it intact to work against the Union drones, making the hardware of the enemy work for the resistance.

Son of a bitch.

A net appeared in the code, strings black against the blue of the virtual sky, arcing through the air toward one of the larger clumps of dragonfly drones. Hayden spun the code through his fingers and tossed up a shield in the wind. The net struck his invisible wall of code and slid down, useless, disintegrating as it went. The drones flew on, and Hayden's shoulders sagged in relief. He felt them, if he concentrated, slumping against the slick fabric of the throne at his back.

The next net came just as fast and, having let his guard down only briefly, he had to struggle to raise a second shield to block it. Hayden knew that if he didn't go on the offense soon any hostiles keeping watch on the battlefield would be able to pick up enough data points to start triangulating his, as yet, hidden position.

Something tickled in the back of his brain, the awareness of danger slicing through the already dangerous streets of the datascape, and Hayden turned in time to see the Asia Prime slinger make her move from the top of a nearby neon encrusted skyscraper.

Sun launched her flatline.exe in the form of a spear—code strung together, reinforced, and hurled forward with tremendous speed, the likes of which no doubt required most of her throne's processing power, enough to make the impact deadly to whatever it struck. It meant that they had more or less decided that simply capturing and retrieving the drones was no longer viable. It would take more force and finely crafted offensive programs to stop one of the state-of-the-art drones. A basic net.exe simply would not do.

From inside MassNet, a slinger could throw out the net.exe and temporarily disable the average drone through the complex web of Wi-Fi signal, broadband, and satellite signals that comprised the complex web of their shared datascape illusion. It was another matter entirely to launch an .exe from MassNet and have the metaphor, and most importantly the program it represented, translate through CodeSource and manifest as an analog strike against the target. To be able to physically damage hostile hardware with a cross-realm assault was a masterful display indeed, and Hayden was begrudgingly impressed.

The slinger steeled himself for what was coming. All thoughts of the Akiaten hacker's influence gone from his mind as the deadly .exe shrieked through the data cascade towards him.

HQ was quiet save for the buzz of whispered conversation that permeated the space whenever a mission was ongoing during regular work hours. The slingers were sequestered away in the lower ground lab, with only a few attendants watching the masters at work, but that didn't mean that no news traveled through the rest of the building.

The slingers who slipped out for coffee offered bits and pieces to the kitchen staff when they asked, updates were then whispered to the dog-tired security operatives who asked for food to be brought to their rooms or their offices. Like rumors traveling through a grade school. It was safest not to send them on their coms or their phones, and they had been warned upon hire that it was grounds for dismissal unless you were transmitting necessary information via a secure, prior approved network.

Phillips had just passed on what he knew to Perada, something with drones, trying to pin down a location for the enemy HQ, whichever one they happened across. There was also a rumor that the drones looked like bugs, but he wasn't too sure about that one. Phillips was of medium height with blond hair buzzed close to his scalp, stationed near one of the several back doors used most often by operatives as they embarked on their missions. There was less chance of the local security cams or enemy surveillance catching them if they used the less conspicuous entrances. Team members who didn't exit and enter dressed in the best body armor money could buy and looked more like civilians, were encouraged to use the front entrance to keep up their ruse of being a functioning apartment building.

The local government, he'd been told, was well aware of their activities and they had yet to attract any noticeable suspicion from the local civilians as well.

It was only just the start of his shift, and, as they wanted to make certain nothing interrupted their current operations, he could expect to be on guard a while longer. Phillips leaned against the wall behind him, looking around for any of his superiors before he did so, then settled in to wait.

In the event of an attack on their base, Phillips was always prepared to hear gunfire, explosions, and echoing screams. However much he daydreamed about having to leap into action on a job, it had never actually happened. They took great care to keep their headquarters hidden from their rivals. In the time he had worked for the Union, he had never fired his gun while on guard duty.

When the alert popped up his heads-up display, the unexpected noise made him fumble to pull up the visual on his HUD. He only needed a second to recognize its significance. He pulled his gun from where it hung on his holster and moved steadily down the hallway toward where the indicator had shown the possible threat on the building plans.

When Phillips rounded the last corner, he found the section of the building that Perada had been assigned to.

At first, he saw nothing, but then he heard the sound of something scrabbling, squeaking against the waxed bright white floor. A few more steps and he saw Perada on the ground, one arm wrapped tight around his gut, blood dripping from his nose to the floor as he struggled to pull himself along.

Phillips saw Perada's gun on the floor, a few scant feet from his grasp, but as he watched, the gun suddenly skittered out of Perada's reach and slid across the floor of its own accord.

His own gun rose in response, but there was no one to shoot. That was a first. The simple absence of a target was suddenly the most terrifying thing he'd encountered. He knew there was something in there with them, some part of his primal self absolutely positive that he and Perada were not alone, and that the enemy was very close.

"Your left!" Perada ground out, jerking his head to one side. Phillips did his best to multitask, following the movement of the man, digging deep into the empty air with searching eyes, and sending out a quick system wide alert, or at least his attempt at one. He was fairly certain he didn't have the clearance needed, but Captain Mitchell would pick it up on the security band and bounce it out on all points.

As the message sent, the air where his gun was trained shimmered and shifted, like water refracting light. Phillips followed the movement with his barrel, noting that it sped up when the assailant realized it had drawn attention. Phillips fired, emptying the magazine of his pistol as he'd been trained, all those years ago in Corsec Academy. He was rewarded with multiple impacts on the shimmering, and now bloody, target. He could see the bullet holes through the cloaking device, the red stained clothing, and the trail left behind on the floor. Perada had reached his gun at long last and began squeezing the trigger of his semi-automatic pistol, several of the bullets slamming into the hostile from behind before the gun went empty and the assailant disappeared around a corner.

Breathing hard, Perada gave him a grin.

The shot came from behind Perada, drilling through the back his head. The air behind him shimmered as he died, his skull neatly cored by a sizeable round.

Phillips felt something blunt and cold strike him from behind. As he slid to the floor, vision darkening, gun tumbling from lax fingers, he counted two more cloaked figures tracking their comrade's blood down the hall.

Laine knew they had followed her as soon as she received the alert. No one else had made the trip from the HQ to the safe-house and back again save for her and the members of security who had gone to clean up the mess of E-Bloc bodies she'd left in her wake.

Even if they had followed one of the security team back in her stead, it still came down to her deciding to take their bait. She could have been more careful, at any given time taking the effort to blank her scent and double back to take a circuitous route back to HQ, and yet she had not.

The hostiles thought they'd sprung a trap within a trap, bringing her to the safe house and then following her back. It was the sort of tactic she'd seen used in other low-grade regions, where cunning took the place of high tech weaponry.

What they didn't know was how experienced she was at suppressing defiance patterns. The loss of Phillips and Perada was tragic though necessary. An acceptable loss recommended by the game theory analytics software that was part of the comprehensive field ops neural package Laine had purchased and installed shortly before being tasked with bringing down Takeda.

To alert Captain Mitchell or anyone for that matter, would have run the risk of her prey sensing the deception. Perada was new to the team, though Laine had known Phillips for a number of years as a site security officer on several field operations. He was a good man, and his death might have caused her grief at some point in the past when she was less than what she was now and the mission took priority.

Captain Mitchell would never authorize such a willful endangerment of Union staffers, which was part of why she was here at Bascilica's request. Alpha augments existed to get things done, which is what led her to the safe house on the edge of the jungle in the first place, and luring the enemy into her lair seemed, to her, the next right thing to do. Let them think they were lions for now.

She tapped her fingers against the blade at her side before adjusting her grip on her rifle and making her way through the chaos that had broken out all over HQ.

There was still a score of slingers downstairs working Nibiru's surveillance project, some processing the heaps of data she was bringing back even as others ran interference as best they could from CodeSource while Hayden played superhero in MassNet.

She hoped there was still security on that floor, or even just one person keeping an eye on their HUD and aware of the danger. Most everyone who was involved with Americana was trained at least to some degree in weapons and rudimentary self-defense, but she knew that very few of them carried weapons, and even fewer did so within the supposed safety of HQ.

When she turned to her left, Mitchell was walking alongside her, half turned toward the back to head off an attack from that direction. He was only wearing his tactical body glove, having perhaps been enjoying some much-deserved rest when the alarm went off, though he had managed to mount a sidearm on his thigh and shoulder his assault rifle. She nodded at him and kept walking. If the Captain had found it odd that she was in full battle dress prior to the attack, he did not make a show of it.

Laine only counted two bodies, and her heads-up display promptly told her that the one closest to the entrance was still breathing. Her enhanced vision was only so helpful in that aspect, but she liked to think this meant that she spotted it sooner, the odd refraction of light in the air, cloaking armor of some sort, much different than the technology embedded in her own. Her armor sufficiently hid her while she remained stationary. Useful enough for recon, but not viable in a firefight. And a firefight was inevitable.

Laine selected semi-auto a millisecond before squeezing the trigger, giving Mitchell a chance to join her in raising his own rifle. Though they both were on semi-automatic, single shot, they went for mag dumps, pumping their fingers against their respective triggers and hurling a blistering salvo of projectiles at the nearly invisible hostile.

Both soldier and operative were firing and moving to put their backs into alignment when it became clear that the enemies they aimed for were anything but easy to track. Even had their cloaking tech failed them, they would have been difficult for anyone without her modifications to hit, no matter how good a shot you were. Hence the full mag dumps, which they focused on the one whose cloaking was already somewhat compromised by battle damage, presumably from the encounter with Phillip and Perada.

Firefights were swift and brutal affairs, and in seconds the bullet riddled corpse of the attacker collapsed to the floor in a ruined heap. The shooters kept up their punishing rate of fire and filled the corridor with projectiles in search of shimmering targets.

It was their movements that gave the other two Akiaten away, fluid, apart from each other but somehow still coordinated. When the quickest one, the one she already dubbed most dangerous in her mind, a calculation run by her analytics and emphatically confirmed by her raw instincts, ran halfway up the far wall, she knew there was nothing they could be but Akiaten. She had already been close to sure, but she could tell that Mitchell knew as well.

She saw a spray of blood that told her one of his bullets had connected. It was only a graze, but the blood-soaked arm became easy to aim for. They continued to pour it on, their Union manufactured extended magazines giving them the sheer ammunition to set about driving the two down the corridor, back the way they had come.

There was a moment, a knife thrown right at the seam of her torso armor and her utility belt, along with bullets coming from more than one direction—where Laine felt something like a ghost of nervousness. The bullets had spanked off of her thick armor, though the multiple impacts drove her back a few steps and sent her crashing into the wall.

The knife, expertly thrown by the dangerous one, had slid into her flesh nearly to the hilt, and the hot static sensation coming from the capacitor in the back of her neck told Laine that her combat efficiency would continue in a steep decline the longer she stayed in the fight.

Both Laine and Mitchell discarded their now empty rifles, choosing to quick draw their sidearms rather than fumble with reloading in the middle of a shootout where there was little to no cover. They kept the Akiaten gunmen at bay, though just barely.

In seconds, there were footsteps behind them, from the stairwell. Some of their security troopers must have finally wised up.

The Akiaten turned tail. Laine and Mitchell and a handful of soldiers following them with a barrage of fire. Somehow, each bullet missed its mark, or, if they hit neither of the resistance fighters was stopping to notice the wounds. They must have been equipped with some armor at least as advanced as her own or were in possession of some other as yet unknown miracles.

The Akiaten hurled themselves out of a third story window, shooting it to pieces as they ran towards it and leaping through them in a shower of safety glass and metal grating. They had barely hit air when a security officer reached the window and fired at them as they soared downwards.

Laine was at the man's side a moment later. Thanks to her ocular augments she was able to witness the Akiaten who'd knifed her, turn his body mid-flight so that he could bring up an automatic pistol, his finger squeezing the trigger as he fell.

Laine grunted and hurled herself backwards, narrowly avoiding the storm of rounds that chewed up the window and interior ceiling.

As she fell back she lashed out with her arm and grabbed the security staffer by his tactical harness to pull him down with her. She hit the floor hard and her vision was a starburst for an instant as her head bounced painfully against the hard floor.

When she shook her senses clear, she saw Mitchell taking a few pot shots out of the window with his sidearm. She could tell immediately from her onboard analytics of the likely position of the enemy and Mitchell's body language that he was more expressing frustration than actually believing he could score a substantial hit.

Laine made to help the security staffer she'd rescued get to his feet, only to see that she'd not rescued him from anything, as he'd taken a round to the neck and one in the face. They must have been gamma loads, as the one that went into his face never came out the other side, instead, bouncing around inside his skull because it could not penetrate the armor of his helmet.

Disappointed in her failed attempt at saving the man's life, Laine had to reassess her opinions on the usefulness of the homemade rounds. These were indeed anything but farmers with a few guns.

Laine waved off medical attention and left the knife where it was as she and Mitchell backtracked to the location where the firefight had begun.

Mitchell stared down at the body of the slain hostile, and at the two dead guards. He nodded, at last, at the fallen Akiaten.

"Call someone to take care of this. I want the body preserved," he said. He turned to the soldiers gathered with them, then, still nervously fingering their triggers. "Lock it down, the whole place. I don't want anyone else in or out until we're certain it's secured. Then, prep all staff for relocation. This place is shot, we've been burned."

He looked to Laine, a more specific order in mind, but found her already gone.

Hayden rubbed the back of his neck. He'd been woken, not so subtly, by Overdog grabbing his shoulder and giving him a shake that nearly pulled him free of the gripping cable in his jack. He'd barely had enough time to avoid Sun's spear before he was unceremoniously pulled out of MassNet, finding himself breathing too fast and shallow in the throne.

His hands shook where they gripped the armrests, it was not pleasant to disengage that abruptly and violently. Frankly, it was nearly as dangerous as getting hit with the full force of a harm.exe. The mind needed time to adjust to a full return to the body.

Across the room, Nibiru still worked tirelessly, fingers clacking on the keys. He glared at Overdog as the man immediately jabbed Hayden's neck with a crash-jet, the pneumatic hypodermic needles that came pre-packaged with a cocktail of drugs and nutrients that would help keep the slinger alive and without cognitive damage after having been torn out of MassNet without proper shutdown procedures. It had always reminded Hayden of how underwater divers who went down deep enough had to make a graduated ascension in order to avoid the nitrogen bubbles in their bloodstream at such depths ripping painfully through their bodies.

The man had better have a damn good reason for so abruptly canceling Hayden's re-match with Sun and putting his body and mind at just as much risk by the hard crash as if he'd already lost to the Prime slinger, not to mention abandoning Nibiru in CodeSource to fend for the drones herself.

Hayden shook his head as the fog of the drugs swept over his mind, dulling the trauma of sudden analog reality even as his body surged with nutrients designed to give him a temporary boost of vitality. He noted the frantic state of things as he peered past Overdog's shoulder at the rest of the operations deck.

All but one of the Union slingers was rushing and back and forth, gathering up their belongings and their personal rigs, while Qais, a relatively average level slinger, had co-jacked with Nibiru and was lending her aide. It was a risky play, allowing another slinger to essentially piggy-back on your mind's processing power and your body's ability to type the code, but at least on the surface, it looked like Nibiru wasn't leaning on the guy too hard.

"Akiaten. Upstairs on the main level. Captain Mitchell just issued a non-essential asset purge and an immediate relocation," growled Overdog as he noticed Hayden's eyes scanning the room. "Sorry about crashing you, no choice, we're moving under guard in twenty minutes. You'll get your shot at Little Miss Sunshine eventually, kid."

"Fuck," Hayden said, his brain still coming down from MassNet, words hard to think of. He pulled the throne's helmet from his head, "I'll get Nibiru."

"Easy cowboy, she's doing fine," Overdog began.

Hayden made himself slide out of the throne and grabbed Overdog's arm. "Sun was working with the E-Bloc cadre, dammit! And that Akiaten slinger is dropping pins on our drones."

Overdog looked ready to argue, but at that moment, everyone's rigs began trilling an alarm and the atmosphere of tension ratcheted up a notch. It had been a day of alarms.

Overdog looked at his display and then at Hayden. "Says Bascilica is setting up a temporary site," he gestured at Qais as the slinger's fingers flew across the keys, his secondary jack, the one usually reserved for MassNet, was plugged directly into Nibiru's rig. "I know he's not you, Cole, but nobody ever will be if they don't step up."

It was scarcely five minutes before she emerged, though it felt like much longer. Overdog insisted that Hayden just stay put, sitting in a chair near the Nibiru and Qais as they worked. It ate at Hayden not to be in the action, being so weak and drugged that he couldn't even help with the asset purge, but even as belligerent as he felt, the man knew deep down that Overdog had done the right thing in crashing him and with the other slinger's help the mousy engineer was holding her own.

Nibiru eventually pulled the cable from her neck and gave Hayden a tired smirk as Qais continued laying traps and shutting doors in CodeSource behind them.

"All the ones that didn't get fried are back," she said. "And the ones that did get fried automatically void their captured data when they malfunction, and they do that by a central processor meltdown. So they won't know what we have, and they won't be able to duplicate the methods we used to make the drones in the first place, those cores burn hot, which is why the drones are so small in the first place, they'll be puddles of slag by the time anyone gets to them analog."

She stopped to catch her breath, leaning heavily on the chair back. Hayden gave her shoulder a weak squeeze. "So, what do we have?"

"Don't know," she answered, looking at the commotion around them. "And I'm guessing we don't have time to look into it. What's going down?"

He told her, realizing that Overdog had blacked her coms while she was jacked in so that she'd be able to focus. It was a patronizing move, but considering she was the new kid on the team, he didn't disagree.

Laine gave chase. And the Akiaten gave her the challenge she craved.

The micro-torch embedded in her left trigger finger had sliced neatly through the thin metal blade of the knife embedded in her waist, which allowed her to empty a full canister of synth-flesh over the base of the blade. The synth-flesh had sizzled at first as it poured over the smoldering blade, though in short order the flesh hardened to the consistency of scar tissue. It looked monstrous. Laine had just crafted a crude lump of flesh around the blade, though it was perfectly functional, as it held the blade in place, keeping it from causing an unmanageable amount of further damage as she gave chase. Laine knew that she was still bleeding internally. She'd have to have all the synth-flesh removed surgically just to get the blade out, but the maneuver reduced the decline in her combat efficiency by at least thirty percent. By her calculations, Laine still had plenty of fight left in her and was determined to share that with her precious new enemies.

Laine's rifle barked in sharp, steady bursts as she pursued the Akiaten, though, at the sheer speeds with which they fled, not to mention their head start, the operative found it difficult pull off a steady, well-aimed shot. She was burning through magazines at a high rate even while just on semi-automatic, and it was her steady stream of fire that prevented the Akiaten from returning fire with much more than hasty shots as they fled.

They dodged her fire when they could and when they couldn't, they twisted their bodies with flips and leaps to turn fatal shots into grazing hits. It was a feat of dramatic significance to an alpha augment with a fortune in accuracy upgrades, but after seeing the movements they made in the process it seemed even more impossible. They wove back and forth with so much frequency and unpredictability that it was difficult for her to get a solid bead on them.

Laine, however, was nothing if not an apex predator, and soon she gave up on actually trying to hit them and focused more on slowing their escape. She swapped out magazines with a fluid grace as she ran, using salvos of deadly projectiles to force the Akiaten to change directions.

On the streets, they had more room to spread out and use the environment to their advantage. They vaulted over walls, swung around street signs, slid across hot car hoods, heat shimmering like the armor they wore.

She imagined she looked fairly insane, sprinting down the street with a gun gripped openly in her hand. Her lungs ached and the city around her looked less familiar. She noted, at one point, a third distortion in the air on the opposite side of the street, but before she could respond the Akiaten cut hard to the right and leaped through the archway of an apartment complex before running across the communal landing.

Laine grunted and hurled herself through the archway, the sudden change in direction causing the blade to shift inside her and shorting out the capacitor in the back of her neck.

Temporarily brought to a stop by the pain, Laine responded by bringing her rifle up to fire at the resistance fighters as they ran, selecting full auto as she traced the enemy with her fire. The Akiaten were impossibly fast, and the hurricane of projectiles Laine sent screaming towards them caused hideous amounts of damage to the apartment complex. The fighters, though, still managed to stay one step ahead of the majority of her bullets. Even the ones that were hit didn't seem slowed down by it.

Laine walked as she fired, using her breath to take control of her pain the old-fashioned way while the capacitor rebooted. The Akiaten vaulted the railing on the opposite end and disappeared down into the street on the other side. Laine grit her teeth and slung her rifle so that she could grip the railing and swing herself over the side and then landing painfully on the ground below.

Civilians ran when they saw her coming. As she pursued the resistance fighters through the city, the crowds grew less and less. They were heading towards the jungle, which suited Laine just fine, as the further out they got the less chance of E-Bloc stormtroopers showing up to ruin a few good kills. She shouldered her rifle after slotting in her last magazine, the weapon's barrel burning hot to the touch, and slid her sidearm from its holster on her thigh.

The amount of blood pouring from the wounded Akiaten made it possible to track them each time she lost sight of the twin shimmers in her oculars.

Mitchell had only grazed one of them, but during the course of her pursuit, she'd managed to score several hits on both of them, though none had been enough to do more than slow them down by increments. She was convinced, by now, that they were augmented in some way. No man could keep up the pace after losing so much blood or sustaining so much damage.

She determined that they had to have some kind of regenerative ability, for even an alpha augment such as herself would be hard pressed to keep up their level of physical exertion while coping with the collective trauma of so many injuries. Her senses were cranked to the max once again, and the headache of the exertion was compounded by the grievous knife wound at her waist, the damage having been made worse by her continued activity.

The red trail increased in amount and frequency each block. They knew and she knew, that even with her enhancements, she would be having a much harder time without it. She had never once underestimated the Akiaten, had not once thought them incompetent.

The figures pulled closer together, the odd effect in the air merging into one larger blob that slowed its progress. When they broke apart, only one kept running forward while the other turned to face her. A sacrificial last stand.

Her respect for them grew, as theirs, no doubt had for her by how relentlessly she'd pursued them. Any organization that bred such loyalty was a worthy opponent, a welcome reward for her reckless bravado.

She could hear the sound of running feet fading, and in front of her, the Akiaten switched off his cloak. She admired him for that. A one on one fight had a code of sorts, and it was an honorable move.

He was lightly armored under an outfit like what Laine imagined was that of a common mega-city thug, with loose fitting clothing, sneakers, and a hoodie, though the bandana he wore to cover his face was anything but, and had the look of being handmade with vibrant colors and patterns.

When he pulled a long balisong style blade from his hip, Laine could not help but gasp, baring her perfect teeth with a feral smile.

She holstered her gun and drew her own weapon, extending the telescoping blade by twelve inches to match the length of her foes.

The Akiaten charged, and Laine met him blade on blade. In the blink of an eye, they exchanged a furious series of slashes, stabs, and parries, each warrior pushing their bodies to the outer edges of their limitations.

Laine's augmented musculature surged with adrenaline, lending yet more power to her blows, and in seconds it was clear that her skill was far beyond that of her opponent. It was only his raw speed and strength that kept him alive, and even so the two deep gashes Laine had opened up on his chest and thigh were draining him of both.

Suddenly he surprised her and instead of making a slash at her throat with his knife, he dropped into a half-hand stand and used his momentum to twist his torso and deliver a crushing heel kick to her waist.

Obviously, the Akiaten knew about the knife wound, and the force of his blow drove the blade yet deeper into her guts. Laine howled in pain and stumbled back as her capacitor blew out again. She managed to get her off hand up in time to block the downward strike from the Akiaten's knife, as the man had spun on the palm of his hand and brought his knife arcing towards her. The blade sank to the hilt through the palm of her hand, and the Akiaten put his full weight behind the knife so that it forced her wounded arm back and drove the point of the blade several inches into her clavicle.

The sensation of the blade scraping against her collar bone was nearly overwhelming, but only nearly, as Laine snarled and pushed the handle of her knife upwards. The operative extended the telescoping weapon as she thrust and the now thirty-two-inch blade shot into the Akiaten's brain from the entry point under his jawline and blasted through the back of his skull.

Laine had only barely noted the beggar when they passed him, ratty shirt and frayed pants, a hat pulled low and a hood pulled over that, casting his face in shadow.

She did not see the shot he fired, only the aftermath. A dart that found a home in the Akiaten's shoulder as she used the point of her blade to swing his twitching body to the side, allowing her to control how the blade in her shoulder moved.

She recognized the sound the gun made, the noise of impact. The Akiaten's body jerked violently as the electricity ravaged his form. It was the sort of weapon that was designed specifically for killing alpha augments, frying the implants, which then worked as wonderful conductors for sending the current through what muscle and bone remained unscathed.

The Akiaten was dead twice over now, the voltage was enough to cook a horse, but his body kept twitching, arms and legs moving jerkily, the rough sidewalk he'd fallen on scraping exposed skin.

Her body turned to where the projectile had come from, knowing that it had been meant for her. Judging from the angle of the shot, her analytics upgrades swiftly determined that the unknown shooter was operating from a vantage point that did not reveal her killing blow to the Akiaten, therefore, the shooter was unprepared for the resistance fighter to suddenly be in the way of the projectile's intended target.

A miss of milliseconds was still a miss.

Laine dropped the blade and went for her gun.

Being a cyberagent herself, if the bullet had found a slot to squeeze through in her armor, or bit into exposed flesh, its effects would be just as deadly to her. Every augment in her body would light up like a lightning rod. Her capacitor, even if it had time to reboot, might have helped her survive the first shot, though she'd be out of action regardless.

Nobody who could score that first shot would hesitate to take a second, or third, to get the job done. The rounds were as expensive as most upgrades, and generally only the most high-end of corporate assassins carried them. A bullet you could use once, an upgrade you could use over and over, so it was only a certain sort who carried them. In the world of cyber agents, such weapons were the nuclear option.

It was only when she turned toward him that she realized the beggar was not a beggar, was in fact, a much bigger threat than the Akiaten had been.

The context clues all fell into place in an instant.

Blending in with the local population, using lightning rounds, the shimmer suit, and simply being able to aggressively track such a high-speed gun battle across the city without registering to the alpha augment's cranked senses and analytics as a threat.

Hirohito.

Laine knew of him from their intelligence files, the lead agent for Asia Prime, an alpha augment, and a passable slinger in his own right.

Laine knew he'd allowed her to run the Akiaten to ground, knew that he'd been watching, and counted herself incredibly lucky that he'd failed to notice the telescoping blade kill before taking his shot. A creature like Hirohito did not miss without being subject to extremely adverse circumstances.

As damaged as she was, Laine knew that she had no hope of besting him in close quarters, and now that he'd adjusted it was unlikely he'd miss with the next lightning round.

Desperate to buy herself some tactical space, Laine raised her rifle with her wounded hand and her pistol in the other, peppering the area with gunfire.

Hirohito had a cloaking device of his own though and disappeared almost as soon as she fired. Laine trained her gun on the quick moving, shimmering form, following him with as much precision as her enhanced vision would allow, which admittedly, was not enough to score a significant hit. She settled for spraying the whole street with rapid fire, peppering signs, crumbling the corners and walls of the old brick buildings that were prominent in this part of the city.

She took fire herself in return, as Hirohito seemed to have slung his assassin's rifle and filled his hand with a sidearm. A few bullets dented her armor, but more often slammed into whatever surface she took cover behind as they did battle in the empty street. A parked car, a garden wall, a fire hydrant that saved her legs from the shot and then exploded outward, shards of yellow metal and a gush of water rising into the air. Perhaps the water soaked his suit, made it start to glitch in and out of true invisibility, perhaps a lucky bullet caught just the right place.

There were a few scattered glimpses of the man in his beggar's attire as he ran, the sleek metal of high-end Asia Prime power armor visible beneath the many holes and tears in the beggar's rags. Each sight of him was eclipsed again when the suit tried to keep functioning. She tracked him with her eyes through the streets until he disappeared midway across a vacant lot and did not surface in her sight again.

Laine breathed a tremulous sigh and ran her fingers over the dents in her suit. One of them was scarcely a full inch from the small vulnerable spot between her neck and shoulder, necessary to give her the mobility she needed. She was seldom so aware of her own mortality.

He had chosen to disengage rather than stay and finish the job, which she knew was well within his power. She was severely damaged, physically exhausted, her headache so powerful from cranking her senses that she was starting to get dizzy, and her ammo was spent down to a magazine and a half of pistol rounds.

It was when the proximity warnings began to blare in her ears and blaze in her HUD that she realized the reason for his choice. E-Bloc response teams were converging on this embattled district, some heading for the Union HQ and others spreading out to cover down on the trail of devastation Laine had left behind her in pursuit of the Akiaten.

The operative slung her rifle into its usual home across her back and bent to retrieve her sword from where she'd left it in the dirt. Her handgun, she left out, just in case Hirohito had the thought to return.

Her eyes scanned the area one last time for shimmering abnormalities before her attention turned to the body of the Akiaten in the street. He'd finally stopped twitching at least. Mitchell would want to see him, would want someone to examine him closely.

The smell of scorched meat caught in her throat as she bent. She took a quick capture, the man had fought as well as any she'd faced, and she wanted to remember the sight. Laine pulled the blade away from her collar bone and slid it into the fighter's hip sheath, and then groaned with effort as she picked up the man's lifeless corpse and heaved it onto her shoulders.

Through her HUD she contacted Mitchell and arranged for extraction, in the process learning where the new HQ was being created. Once the Captain sent her the coordinates Laine set off, her augmented muscles straining with the effort of running with a dead body over her shoulders, but fueled by the certainty that this island mission was guaranteed to have a one hundred percent yield of either death or glory. For the alpha augment, it felt as if enlightenment itself lay hidden somewhere in those extremes.

10

The thing laid out on the table wasn't human, even if it closely resembled one. Biology wasn't exactly Hayden's area of expertise, and the corpse was ravaged by bullets, blade, and electrical trauma, but even he could recognize that.

Close-up, the Akiaten looked off, but that was it as far as Hayden could see. He had seen that much himself during their battle with E-Bloc on the street. Laine, however, had danced a full tango with several of them and had much to say of their prowess. There was something strange in the way they moved she'd said, closer to an animal, some agile jungle cat than a human would ever come.

He and Laine had talked about it at length the first full day after HQ had been attacked and then abandoned four days ago. She and Mitchell had been closer to them than anyone else save for the couple of guards who'd met their end just as the alert was sent out. They had lived to write their experiences and opinions in the reports that Bascilica asked for. The alpha augment's report was filled with the kind of poetic slant that Hayden was used to, perhaps even more so this time, and the slinger suspected that it was because the alpha augment was confined to HQ.

Laine was so badly damaged that even she didn't protest when the Captain put her on recovery lockdown. She wasn't even allowed to wear any of her kit, restricted to basic body glove only. Hayden suspected that the Captain and Laine would get a major ass-chewing from Bascilica about the cost of her repairs, both cyber and organic.

Even looking at the Akiaten now, Nibiru's autopsy long complete, the sight of the body unnerved Hayden on a rather primal level. There was nothing so obviously spooky in its outward appearance, at least not when it was still. Hell, the fact that he thought of it as an 'It' and not a 'him' was telling.

Hayden had just finished reading the write up that Nibiru had sent him, and he knew what lay within. Muscle tissue tightly packed beyond normal human limits and the ligature to support it, enlarged lungs and heart that perhaps explained their incredible stamina, and a skeletal structure that differed just enough from that of normal humans to raise brows.

A human in the naked eye but a monster now revealed in the measurements. The cells they had extracted, no matter where on or in the body they came from, were poised for mutation. Nibiru had gone on a tangent about the camouflage cells one found in an octopus, explaining the comparison with wide eyes while Hayden did his best to follow along. It wasn't often that he was unfamiliar with technical terminology, but he'd had to remind Nibiru midway through that this was his first alien autopsy.

She was still glaring at him for that.

Perhaps it was distasteful to make jokes while leaning over a dead body, regardless of the type of body it was. Honestly, it still creeped him out more than a little that the unassuming and youthful engineer also happened to be a third-degree medical student. That was several degrees away from professional grade, but more than enough to make her a functional field medic and forensic coroner.

Hayden started to wonder if he needed to go back to school, as he was starting to feel like he'd been resting on his slinging laurels and spending his money while youngsters like Nibiru were cross-training on their way up the corporate ladder.

The skin of the chest had been fused back together. Unlike stitching, it left behind only a thin red line in its wake. Hayden couldn't say he was upset that he'd missed the actual blood and guts, but the pictures Nibiru included with the report may as well have been the same. He knew little about what it was supposed to look like, but from the look of concern on her face and the introspection in Laine's eyes, he would guess nothing normal. All viscera looked the same to him, but he took them at their word. Nibiru had studied this sort of thing, knowing how different parts fit together was kind of in her job description and she knew when things looked off. He supposed Laine had also seen more than her fair share of bodies. Being one of the Union's top slingers meant he rarely got close enough to the street level violence to experience such things in volume.

"I'm not sure what to make of it," Nibiru mused, breaking the silence as always. "Either they aren't human, which is insane, or they've been bio-modified past the point where they're recognizable as our species. I mean, once you open them up, of course."

Laine, Hayden noted, looked oddly thoughtful at this, her face seeming to soften around the edges as she stared at the body on the metal slab. It figured she would feel a sort of kinship with the Akiaten. Hayden had never thought of Laine as caring about the differences, the upgrades and the cybernetics that kept her separate, but now that he considered it, her attempts to connect were obvious. The strained smiles she gave were a mimicry of what she saw the people around her exchange, a perfect copy on the surface, but with something missing at its core.

"Did you understand it?" Nibiru continued. "The report, I mean. Did it make sense?" She looked down at the body as she spoke, following Laine's gaze.

Hayden shrugged. "As much as someone like me can understand something like this. Not exactly my territory."

Nibiru snorted. "Come on Cole. It's not mine either. I have training sure, but I'm much more used to slicing up things of the mechanical variety."

"Well," he said, "It looks like you did a good enough job to me."

Laine looked up at last, as though she'd only just noticed the conversation taking place in the vicinity. She turned her gaze to the young engineer and tried on a smile once more. It was as off-putting as the rest of them, but there was something earnest in the attempt, even if it was like a crocodile attempting the expression. "It's more than adequate, Nibiru. I'm sure Bascilica will accept it."

"Not sure how he'll take the news," Hayden said. "You sent it already?"

She nodded. "I messaged it to the whole team at once. Figured the faster I broke it, the faster we could move on."

Laine circled the table the body lay on, leaving the conversation as abruptly as she'd entered it. Nibiru looked to Hayden in uncomfortable amusement as the operative circled the body like a predator looking for the best place to strike.

"There's energy still inside it," she assessed. "I can feel it niggling at my implants, like a surge in the power grid."

Hayden couldn't keep the incredulous look off his face, but Nibiru was nodding. "There are some freaking weird readings on the instruments I used to check the blood," she said, nodding at Laine. "I'll show you."

Having had enough of blood and bodies, Hayden left them to it and went into the corridor outside to find his way to the new operations deck and set up his rig. He would prefer working in a room without a recently dead body that still, apparently, contained energy of some sort. He'd hate to be immersed in CodeSource if it rose from the table, and the fact that his imagination was going in that direction was enough to make him keep walking.

Nibiru and Laine joined him shortly after, just as he prepared. It wasn't his usual set up. The new HQ was smaller than the old and had a temporary feel to it, as though everyone inside were simply waiting for the hammer to drop and the order to come to pack up again. The entire base of operations being compromised was a rare happening, and all the staff seemed wary to settle in again.

In a single conflict, Union Americana had ended up the third player in this contest for the nexus, and none of the staffers, including himself, were used to or content with being the outliers in this corporate struggle. They'd been burned and burned hard. It was going to take precious time for the group to come together as a team once more and get back to the business of winning.

Laine laid out her own findings on the table before him, readouts of chemical residue and micro-fibers. Hayden wasn't an expert in forensics any more than he was in autopsies and what they entailed. *Damn, even the killer was cross-trained, he really needed to get his act together*, but he did know how to run a comprehensive search in CodeSource and that was what he did.

He jacked in and crossed the given information with other things, bloodstains, bullets, the Akiaten's known patterns of travel that Laine had picked up during her operations.

Maybe he was feeling threatened, or wanted to show off, but whatever the reason, Hayden launched a major data sweep. The code cascaded across his senses as the slinger hacked through the weak firewalls of the local government that, as of yet, remained independent of corporate influence. He pulled at the strings of spyware he'd left in competitor databases here and there over the years, and even went so far as to boldly (and without backup or authorization from Overdog or the Cap) slice a few files from E-Bloc's lesser defended redundant storage systems that had been co-opted from civilians and the parts of the government they had influence over. All of that combined with the Union's extensive information collective made for a rather comprehensive dragnet.

Nibiru's drone swarm may not have had a chance to secure any clues as to the energy source or its nexus, but what they had provided was a vast database of minute details about much of the city that surrounded them. While the surveillance grids that Hayden sliced might not have the level of sophistication to tie all the details together, his own rig ran the correlations against what the drones had secured, and a pattern began to emerge.

It appeared that Nibiru's drone run was not the abysmal failure they thought it had been; in fact, it had given the Union a powerful surveillance database.

It didn't take long to find something worth the monumental effort, which was good, as he knew that Overdog would eventually have a chance to go through the service logs and he'd get busted pretty hard for slicing without backup. He recorded the coordinates in his HUD before his brain could lose them.

He'd been out of commission for forty minutes, long enough that Nibiru had left to talk the kitchen out of some food. Laine was simply staring at him as he came back to himself, as though she hadn't taken her eyes from his work during the entire ordeal, and perhaps she hadn't. They'd been working together long enough he had no doubts that she knew he was making a play.

As he plugged the analog coordinates of what he'd found into his rig, she moved closer so she could better see the small complimentary display on his rig. In turn, he angled his screen a bit to better accommodate her as he slowly eased himself out of CodeSource.

Americana owned their fair share of satellites positioned around any of their given mission sites, allowing them to run coordinates instantaneously. While they might not be able to just pinpoint the as yet undiscovered energy nexus, they were exceptionally accurate otherwise. It also contributed to the ease with which they kept track of their operatives and scoped out potential strategic locations, such as the new HQ they were still settling in to. The locals they'd recruited from the government and civilian real estate industry had done their best on short notice for the new HQ. The picture on the screen zoomed in, at Hayden's insistence, to the point that he and Laine could easily make out buildings, street sign names, and even a list of traffic cams that Hayden could slice from CodeSource and use for eyes should they have the need to do so.

The neighborhood it showed them was nearly as run down as the rest of the city that existed outside the concentrated wealth of the glittering city center. He noted that the people wandering through did not look quite as bad off as some of the people they encountered outside both the previous HQ and their current location. The buildings were brightly colored, as though they'd been painted sometime in the last decade and there were more than a dozen stalls lining the streets with vendors seemingly hacking out prices in the air between them. It was near to the water, docks were visible depending upon which camera angle Hayden chose, and the fare seemed to be predominantly seafood and related items.

"Fish market bourgeoisie? Hayden suggested with an attempt at levity. "I'd say this place damn near passes for middle class, by local standards."

Nibiru re-entered the room, dropping three plates on the table, still steaming. The food was styled after the local cuisine even though it mostly consisted of pre-packaged military grade meals with a side of plantains, a common enough item in this part of the world, though whether that was a result of the emergency relocation affecting their kitchen supply logistics or a choice made by the culinary staff was anybody's guess.

Hayden watched Laine's eyes narrow in surprise or suspicion the food, as though she hadn't thought to be included whenever Nibiru announced she was bringing the meal back.

Nibiru, for her part, seemed to think nothing of it, as she smiled at the pair. She stood behind Hayden, peering over his shoulder as she ate a bite of fried plantain she'd snatched from one of the plates. "What about the fish market?" she asked, around the food.

"This is where the combination of factors has led us," Laine said. "The only place in the city with a large concentration of the fiber, the blood, and the chem-trail that coordinates in any way with our preconceived paths for them. Only place that makes sense."

Nibiru lifted a shoulder, slid down into the seat. "It strikes me as a tragedy that the surveillance capacities of corporations and governments are as advanced here as they are in first world nations and yet everything else is still so third world bootleg.

"It is the priority of those in power to stay in power," responded Laine almost off-handedly, "I am surprised to see resistance activity in a less impoverished district, that indicates a larger network of sympathizers than initial estimations."

"Well, it's inconspicuous enough for anyone not working with the volume of data we've been able to collect from engaging them. You've got to give them points for that," said Hayden with a mischievous grin. "Though E-Bloc loses points since they've been street fighting these guys for weeks without pinning them down."

"How many hard-wired cameras do we have access to?" Laine questioned. Hayden could already see her mapping the area in her head.

He swept his hand at the screen. "There are three in the area, it's not a complete shit-hole like the district our last HQ was in, but it's further from the city's center, less wired. There's no audio on the camera feed either. We could probably set some up, but we'd have to send someone in for that, and there's no point since we'll be going in regardless. Here's the thing about the cameras though, after that Akiaten slinger went beast mode on E-Bloc I have to say I wouldn't trust any hardware that's not our own. The slinger could have left a trace program or maybe even a tripwire.exe that could fry whoever is trying to slice the hardware."

"I think it looks all right, the neighborhood you know," Nibiru said absently, still eating, her gaze switching back and forth from the display on Hayden's computer screen and her own HUD, where he figured she had pulled up the autopsy report once more. "Our own standards of niceness are probably way out of proportion. Looks nice compared to most places here. Like you said, third world bourgeoisie, but for them, there's no comparison."

She was right. The streets shown by the cameras were free of the potholes and crumbling sidewalks that littered the other parts of the city and there was noticeably less damage and graffiti marring the shells of the buildings. Pretty decent place for a safe house, just a quiet unassuming trade district.

Hayden nodded once to show his acquiescence. "Alright," he said. "It's better than 'not a complete shithole.'" He saved the coordinates along with the information that had led him there to a file—sent copies to both Laine and Nibiru so they could easily access them themselves, and then to Bascilica and Captain Mitchell.

"It won't be long now and it will look more like the hood we just left," he said, "If things go south with a bullet."

Laine bared her teeth in anticipation.

Nibiru stood, wiped her hands on her pants, and began walking back to the morgue. "If you'll excuse me, I'm gonna tuck this guy back in."

Having never seen the engineer in a firefight, Hayden was glad she was sitting this one out. He had no doubt that she could hold her own, but he had grown to think a lot of the young woman in the time they'd worked together. Intimate relationships were against protocol for this very reason and he wasn't sure he would be able to keep his attention where it should be unless he knew she was out of harm's way. He was getting too fucking sentimental, and they weren't even sleeping with each other.

Get it together Cole.

Nibiru could be helpful enough from HQ if they had need of her prowess in CodeSource, and she could back up the other slingers like Qais just fine, though he hoped they weren't in dire enough straits to actually need her.

It had been quite a while since he had needed to suit up himself for a field op. His armor still fit him well, which he took as a positive sign that all the snacking he'd done on the local food hadn't had too much of an effect.

Slinging, especially in MassNet with your brain going full speed, burned an unbelievable number of calories, and it wasn't uncommon to emerge from the sleep one needed afterward completely ravenous. He could have used something else to eat just then, the kitchens had been struggling to put together anything semi-edible with the rudimentary supplies they had been saddled with since they moved into headquarters. The plates that Nibiru had brought to him and Laine earlier had tasted like the bland, rehydrated food you might expect on a military operation. It was plain that it had been stocked with emergencies in mind and little else.

Nibiru hadn't seemed to mind it, but she didn't seem the type to complain about something that couldn't be changed. Laine, he knew, thought of food as fuel to keep her moving and little else. He was sure that with her modifications, she didn't even need as much as she ate, it was just her way of keeping up the illusion of humanity, of trying to fit. He really should have eaten more, maybe his high-profile status really was making him soft, when he'd been a rookie slinger any calorie was a good calorie.

However well the armor fit him and however strong it was, it felt strange to wear it again. It had been a few years since he entered the field for something other than slipping out to sample the local food, and armor never occurred to him when he was marching on his stomach. The last few jobs had not required it, he'd simply done his usual slinging, and, on a few occasions, watched Laine's back or their trooper's movements through CodeSource.

He stepped into the boots that fused to the rest of his suit and equipped the custom sidearm Laine had commissioned for him years ago, hidden beneath the rest of his suit. Most of the slingers weren't issued firearms, but being one of the top hackers for the Union had more than a few perks, and one of them was an open-ended carry license.

Hayden's biometric chip was calibrated to allow him to access and use any and all Union firearms he was willing to achieve a basic training grade on. Hayden had never bothered to get graded on anything but a pistol, a fact that had seemed to annoy Laine enough that she'd insisted on gifting him with the mother of all pistols. That suited Hayden just fine, as he'd not been to a range in months, so the target finder and extended mag would come in useful if they got into trouble.

They took a van to the market. With the Akiaten slinger at large there was no telling what systems and hardware might be compromised, and in the heat of the moment, Hayden might be called upon to jack into CodeSource for some combat slicing.

It was in those moments, when the slinger was struggling to pull off a righteous hack even as the bullets were flying, that it took a hardened professional like Hayden to do the coding and a combat operative to keep him alive while exposed. He didn't know and didn't want to know just how many people Laine had put down while standing over him on this mission or that as he was in the coding trance.

The exterior of the van was armored but didn't look it. The metal of the doors and the hood were made from a similar if differently constructed material as that of their armor. He had been assured, when he was picked up from the airport in a similar vehicle, that the darkly tinted glass was shatterproof.

Mitchell was sending him and Laine with two other security operators. The first, a redheaded woman who was taller than the man at her side, designated herself the driver. She climbed behind the wheel and Laine joined her in the front seat. The two seemed to know each other, and though Laine's conversational skills were slightly strained as always, they kept up a running back and forth on the different strategies for the mission and subsequent extraction should things go wrong.

The second operative, a man with close cropped dark hair and a darker demeanor, seemed content enough to ignore Hayden, who was fine with the silence and alternated between listening to Laine and the driver speak and skimming through the files available in his HUD.

It wasn't an excessively long trip, nor was the traffic terrible. It was the route that made things drag. The operative behind the wheel took a long, complex path that involved a good deal of backtracking and crossing their own tracks. Toward the end, Hayden was sure that they had passed HQ on three separate occasions.

It was perhaps his nerves that made the journey drag. When he checked the time, it had not yet been twenty minutes.

Hayden had always enjoyed a complex relationship with chronological time, given the fact that on an average day he spent most of his waking hours plugged into CodeSource or MassNet. If he wasn't plugged into one or the other and coursing through the data at blinding speeds he was spending his money on this vice or that, living as hard and fast in analog reality as he did in the digital.

All slingers worth their wires struggled this way, though that knowledge didn't make it any easier to sit still and count the seconds, knowing that if he'd been plugged in his mind would have reached the target in seconds.

By the time the van reached its destination, the female operative had turned the conversation to the security measures being taken to keep the new HQ under the radar. She eased the car into a secluded space behind an abandoned stall.

It was near dark and the market was beginning to clear, people leaving, arms laden with baskets and bags of whatever they'd seen fit to buy. The last few vendors had begun to gather up their wares and store them away, or else, prepared to push their smaller carts to wherever they left them at night.

Some of them looked heavy and Hayden winced to see an elderly, frail looking man struggle to pull his cart along. Third world bourgeoisie indeed, or his own ideas about how things worked, as such a sight would never be seen in most places Hayden frequented, as there would be cargo drones and assistance freelancers everywhere.

Hayden shifted impatiently as he waited. He wasn't much for surveillance when it was occurring somewhere other than the datascape and he found himself eager to get out and get the mission underway.

It hadn't been long after Nibiru's autopsy and the subsequent message containing the coordinates of the Akiaten's most likely location that Bascilica had ordered the mission. Their superior wanted it done so quickly that there was no time for the usual pre-deployment briefing with Captain Mitchell, just an alert to join Laine immediately in the parking garage and wait for orders.

Apparently, Bascilica knew enough not to dispute the importance of Nibiru's findings and was smart enough, or scared enough, to realize the importance of gathering more information on their enemy, especially now that the Akiaten were confirmed metahumans enhanced with bio-ware rather than cyberagents with insanely advanced tech upgrades. It was worth further investigation just for that fact.

Nibiru had wanted to deploy the dragonfly drones as an added surveillance tool, but Basilica and Hayden both had argued against it. If things went poorly on the ground, the last thing anyone wanted was an attack coming from the datascape or the loss of more of the costly drones. This was an analog mission all the way unless Hayden was called upon to slice local hardware, hence his presence in the van. They had to handle this Akiaten situation before it escalated much further and truly hampered their ability to search for the nexus. The constant struggle against the other corporations had already fragged their mission timeline. Pressure had to be relieved somewhere.

The real interest though lay in the fact that, with such advanced bio-ware, it was likely that the Akiaten were already more than capable of harnessing the energy emanating from the pulse.

It was just a theory, but there was every chance that the Akiaten knew exactly where the nexus lay and how to reach it. Even if they didn't yet know how to harness or control it properly, Hayden had no doubt that they were at the very least in the process of figuring it out. How else to explain the presence of both a strange new kind of power and metahumans in the same out of the way, formerly inconsequential region of the post-war world?

A handful of the civilians leaving the market passed by too close to the van for comfort. Hayden knew the windows were tinted too darkly to see through, but he averted his eyes anyway and gave the reinforced shirt he wore a nervous tug.

The armor they all wore was a relatively new, clever invention, it had the appearance of plainclothes, normal outfits, jeans, shirts, button-down, suit jackets, but had nearly half the strength and defensive ratings as the armor Laine and the other operatives would wear on a mission where covertness was a less important concern, and that was not insignificant.

It looked normal enough, but it still felt enough like armor that Hayden knew his movements when he wore it were on the sluggish side. There was a weight and a sturdiness that would not be felt with actual plainclothes. He would have preferred straightforward armor, of which he had his own, rarely used set as well, but the area was public, however thin the lessening crowd, and he understood the need to keep a low profile after the chaos of the past week.

His sidearm melded neatly into the side of the shirt he wore, the seam allowing him to keep track of its placement. He could feel the cold weight of it against his lower ribs, pressing into his hip bone when he leaned against the door.

Just when Hayden thought they'd be spending the rest of the night in the van, the sun lowered itself enough that the operatives felt confident in vacating the vehicle.

He got out on his own side, walking alongside Laine while the other two operatives paired up ahead of them. It had been a while since his last jaunt in the field, but not so long that he had forgotten how it worked. While this wasn't specifically a combat op, it *was* a close quarters recon so it could easily turn to combat. He kept his hand away from his weapon, as gripping at something hidden on his hip would only look suspicious, but still close enough that he could reach it easily.

He matched Laine's steps and watched her body language from the corner of his eye, ready to respond if he saw her tense or reach for her own weapons. Her lockdown had been lifted, though he could tell she was still feeling the effects of her protracted combat against the Akiaten and then the legendary operative Hirohito. Of course, Laine on her worst day was still twice the killer he would ever be on his best day.

The four of them didn't walk in tight formation, but rather like a group of workers on their way to a job or from one. Their implants and clothing made them look enough like tech elites from the rather multi-cultural Manila city center that Hayden wasn't anticipating trouble on the approach. Still, they were a bunch of Union operatives, and as inconspicuous as they did their best to be, it wouldn't take but a second glance for the locals to distinguish the operatives from locals. While such a sight would be out of place in this (whatever Nibiru said) slightly less shitty part of the city, they were still less conspicuous than they would have been in combat armor.

Laine still walked like a soldier, like something hunting prey, but there was nothing to be done about that.

Hayden had already confidently identified which building to recon. The hack he'd done back at HQ had led him to a more specific locale than the fish market at large. The coordinates zeroed in on a certain warehouse, and the location matched the municipal data he'd sliced from the government's system as well. He'd had to be careful with that one, half afraid that E-Bloc had already hacked their system and left a trap ready to close on him or a tag ready to attach itself to his IP.

The four of them stuck together, though in a loose group, as they walked across the street. They were close enough to the water that, though Hayden couldn't quite see it, he could smell salt in the air. They turned onto a smaller street, uphill, closing in on the target building.

The door was in sight when the armored truck roared up.

Gunfire spewed from the mounted gun on the top of the truck like fire from the mouth of a volcano and troopers in E-Bloc issued armor poured from the back door. The truck had parked across the square for some strategic reason that Hayden didn't understand.

Though the square held only a scant number of people, there were more than enough in the center and scattered throughout the perimeter of the market to create an obstacle for the soldiers trying to reach their objective as they divided into two squads.

Instead of adjusting their movements to accommodate the civilians, the E-Bloc soldiers plowed through, the tactical shields affixed to their forearms easily bashing people out of their way. They forced their way through vendors hauling their wares home and shoved aside mothers towing their children.

Hayden almost managed to convince himself that the shooting didn't start until the soldiers were clear of the civilians. He pushed the sight of the mounted gun on the truck out of his mind as if attempting to deny the harsh reality of it, but he saw blood on the sidewalk from a few individuals unlucky enough to catch what he truly hoped were stray bullets. The panic in the air was palpable.

E-Bloc had clearly had more than enough of the Akiaten resistance, and it appeared that they considered the locals no better than sympathizers. The locals scattered in every direction made all the more frantic as the troopers adjusted their course every few seconds as if anticipating return fire from whoever was inside the building.

Laine had already turned towards the chaos and he knew she was running the analytics as the other operatives scrambled for cover and attempted to stay blended in with the locals.

Hayden followed the alpha augment's lead as she nudged him toward the stalls along the street, where scant cover might be found. Laine then started forward, deploying her gun with practiced ease and releasing a volley of fire that tore into the trooper operating the mounted gun, sending him falling back inside the armored vehicle.

Hayden fumbled for his own gun and moved steadily to the side, the security operatives moving with him, dutifully shielding him with their own bodies. This was supposed to be close quarters recon, and they'd had about five seconds of that before E-Bloc ruined everything. At this point, protocol was for immediate exfiltration back to their van, so obviously, their loose cannon had to join the gunfight.

Though several of the E-Bloc soldiers returned fire at Laine when she started, their fire pinging off of their own armored truck as she ducked behind it, the bulk of them seemed interested in the same building that Hayden and his crew had been targeting for intelligence.

Several squads swept through the doors, shooting out the hinges as they approached and using their shields to batter them open so that the troopers could rush inside with guns up. Screams leaked out through the open windows and a cacophony of gunfire reverberated through the square. Perhaps they were Akiaten inside because someone was shooting back. Perhaps most of them had already taken a tunnel or a back door to safety at the sound of the first shot and it was just a rearguard of resistance fighters buying their comrades time with their own lives.

Whatever the case, the only people Hayden saw coming out of the side door that suddenly opened into an alley he could see from his vantage point across the street were civilians, limping and bleeding, and it made his stomach clench with a mix of guilt and rage.

E-Bloc, it seemed, was not interested in taking prisoners.

Hayden breathed hard and felt the slight shift in the weapon as he thumbed off the safety, his finger flexing on the hot trigger as his mind raced nearly as fast as his heart.

11

The streets were a violent and chaotic mess. Once Hayden was secured behind a small car parked on the opposite side of the street, the security operatives had moved on to helping Laine neutralize as much of the E-Bloc threat as they could. They, like Laine and Hayden, were only equipped with sidearms, so Hayden wasn't sure how much progress they were making on that front.

Perhaps they hoped to mix things up enough with the troopers that they could coax Laine out of the fight and back into a more appropriate extraction pattern. Americana's small, in and out team was certainly outnumbered, and even with the presence of Laine, it was suicide to think they could decisively engage E-Bloc at this point.

At least, Hayden thought, it seemed that the antics and maneuvers of his own team had provided some of the local civilians with the needed distraction to get themselves out of harm's way. They stuck to the empty food stalls and scant few parked cars the same way he now did, using them as a path of sorts, to run through as they escaped the bullets' reach. Of course, it also helped that now E-Bloc had an enemy in the vicinity both inside the building and out in the streets who was actually shooting back, they seemed less and less concerned with using said civilians as target practice.

Even so, Hayden could hear the screams and the gunfire still coming from the building that both his own team and the E-Bloc troopers had apparently targeted. There was no way of knowing if Akiaten were actually inside as they had thought, but the sounds leaking through the shattered windows and the bloodied, panicked batches of locals skittering out the back and side doors told him that things were going poorly for everyone in there.

With the mix of gunfire, shouted orders, and panicked yells, it was difficult to pick one sound out among the orchestra, but one new noise stole the bulk of his attention, all his senses focusing. This scream was high and rising into a wail; when his eyes found the source, a child frozen in the center of the marketplace, Hayden felt himself rise from his crouch nearly involuntarily. There wasn't much of a decision-making process, nor a dramatic moment of hesitation. He simply stood and began to move. Had he paused to think, to weigh the options, he might not have gone, and yet here he was, sprinting across open ground during a firefight. It was sentimental, foolhardy, and the only decent thing to do.

Perhaps, when seeing a something small and helpless in peril, some primitive part of the brain overrode all else. It was simpler than that though—Hayden knew. He saw the kid with tears streaming down his face, big dark eyes, and curly hair, face steadily growing redder as he cried, as though he were angrier at losing track of his family than frightened of the flying bullets.

Hayden felt a twinge of guilt for his part in putting these people in danger and even a spark of anger that there was danger to put them in in the first place.

You're losing your edge cowboy, he thought to himself in Overdog's voice as he sprinted, *in the old days you'd have stayed pro and focused on saving your own hide.*

His gun in his hand, Hayden made his way into the street. His progress was slowing, despite his sudden burst of courage, as he entered the kill zone. He didn't have the blend of confidence and experience that Laine or the operatives did, that allowed them to go sprinting into gunfire with what appeared to be scarcely a thought to their own safety. Even knowing that his armor would protect him from all but the harshest of penetrating weapons, it was difficult to make himself voluntarily leave the cover the overturned carts from food stalls provided. He did his best to stick to them where he could, trying to keep himself covered from at least one side as he ran.

On one of his several pauses, he caught the red-headed operative looking at him with one eyebrow raised, either impressed that he'd joined the fighting or wondering what the fuck a slinger was doing acting as though he were a combat operative himself. Whatever her reasoning, Hayden was relieved as she began to make her way toward him, drawing fire away from him as she did so.

Better her than him, he thought to himself. He crossed one last narrow open space, pulse pounding so hard that he could feel it any given part of his body. He could hear it in his ears and feel it in the too tight grip of his hand around the loaded gun he still held. When he was finally close enough to reach the kid with one more sprint, he decided he'd taken more than enough time already, and that the kid had likely used up his fair share of good luck at this stage. To wait for the operative to come close enough to give him proper cover was tempting fate.

He worried as he rushed forward, that he should have first put his gun away. He wasn't sure if he could hold a kid and aim at the same time should the situation call for it, having never had occasion to try. He guessed that target finder was going to come in handy after all.

This wasn't exactly the sort of scenario Union Americana went over in the rudimentary weapons training they made sure all prospective employees passed, whatever their rank or station in the company. It wasn't like the corporation felt that slingers needed close protection training, that was for the ones protecting the slingers.

The boy, Hayden was sure, couldn't have been more than five or so, and when Hayden scooped him up, he found himself shocked by the lack of weight. He didn't exactly have a wealth of experience with children, they weren't a common sight given his lifestyle choices, and he had little enough to do with them in the Union, much less outside the confines of the corporation.

The boy came along easily enough, seeming to recognize that, whoever Hayden was, he meant well. The child locked both arms tight around Hayden's neck, his grip surprisingly strong, and held on as Hayden began to make his way back the way he'd come. The slinger saw no way he could easily make it back to the perimeter of the market where he'd started, now that a few of the E-Bloc troopers had gotten wise to his path, but he could at least get the boy to some semblance of cover elsewhere.

Stupid analog reality, Hayden raged, if this was datascape and the kid a piece of data or software package he'd have dropped a baffle.exe before rushing in, smacked anybody in his way with a boot.exe, and maybe left a tripwire.exe behind him on his way to a friendly network and eventual exit.

There would be a few high fives from the other slingers and a big bonus he could spend chasing the kinds of women who didn't play for free, but this wasn't the datascape, and here he could only move as fast as his legs could carry him.

Now I'm gonna die saving some random kid, fumed Hayden, cursing his own basic humanity as he decided to at least shoot something before getting hollowed out by E-Bloc bullets. He'd only just adjusted his hold on the kid so he could swing his pistol around when the level of chaos increased by several more increments.

Akiaten, moving alone or in pairs, were making their way out of the surrounding buildings. Some headed to the marketplace, while others moved for the targeted building, both of which were still thick with E-Bloc troopers and civilians.

The E-Bloc troopers looked unavoidably panicked at their appearance, as if they'd been expecting to slaughter sympathizers and neutralize a significant part of the resistance support network, to send a message about what happens to those who aided the resistance, not to engage the actual fighters themselves. Their squads had spread themselves thin, expecting little resistance and already finding more than they had bargained for in the presence of Laine and the two security operatives.

The Akiaten began firing, fighting, immediately. Their movements were coordinated and yet still fascinatingly individual, with no two maneuvers being the same as they poured over railings, leaped across rooftops, and vaulted parked cars as if they provided little obstacle to their motion. Their movements were almost hypnotic in their grace and complexity.

Even so, as the local warriors fired, few eyes lingered on the movement of the Akiaten as everyone, combatant and bystander alike, scrambled to adjust. One group of Akiaten moving down the center stalls had one member who simply walked ahead, massive patchwork machine-gun sweeping from side to side, firing gamma loads whenever an E-Bloc trooper reared their head, while another ran down the railing of a nearby walkway, and another still leaped over it.

Laine continued her assault of the armored vehicle, having used her elbow to smash through the supposedly shatter-proof viewport on the near side of the vehicle. After having poured a full magazine from her sidearm into the vehicle through the port, she slapped another in and racked the slide just in time to gun down a trooper at point-blank range as he rushed around the side of the truck.

Her small caliber rounds might not have done much more than drive the truck crew out of their vehicle and into the open, but at such close range, her rounds punched through the trooper's armor in several places. She sprinted around the other side as another followed his comrade, and sent him to the ground with a kick in a weak spot that made his leg bend the wrong way in the center before pushing the barrel of her pistol under his thick helmet's visor and pulping his skull with two rounds.

Hayden's ears tuned in on the noise and he heard the crunching sound even through all the shots being fired and the sound of a grenade going off in the distance.

The kid pressed his face into Hayden's shoulder as the slinger ran, spraying troopers with suppressing fire, and kept it there as if it would make a difference. Hayden was glad the kid didn't see Laine execute the trooper.

After catching the slinger's eye and giving him a curt nod, Laine turned and fired the remnants of her magazine at the Akiaten and the E-Bloc squad still struggling to own the street, her small caliber rounds not doing much at this range other than antagonizing both factions. Then she jumped back into cover behind the truck, dodging shots fired from each side so that they slammed into the other, her presence helping them damage each other faster. She swiftly reloaded and emerged once more, seemingly intent on repeating the maneuver, successfully distracting everyone from Hayden as he moved.

Watching Laine at work always felt like watching a top-notch film to Hayden. He scrambled to reach cover while the alpha augment distracted everyone. Her movements were smooth enough to seem almost choreographed, the position of each limb carefully considered, her shots timed to match the decisions and incremental leanings of her foes. There was nothing but satisfaction on her face when she killed, no trace of disgust or niggling guilt. It always looked, like Laine herself, a bit too polished and cold to be real. The only thing that, sometimes, looked on the offside of perfect, was the way she focused a disproportionate amount of her attention on the bodies as they dropped and the blood that poured out afterward, spreading out beneath them like a crimson shadow.

Hayden was still pinned down in no-man's-land, neither of the two armies paying him much attention. He imagined he looked like a civilian himself, dressed in what appeared to be plainclothes and holding a child and scampering from pitiful scrap of cover to pitiful scrap of cover. They probably hadn't even noticed when he'd hosed down an E-Bloc trooper only moments before, as there was so much crossfire going on he doubted anyone had a clear picture of the battle as a whole.

That was the thing about firefights, all chaos, and madness until everyone on one side was dead or had enough and retreated. He imagined he looked more concerned than threatening. It was only the gun in his hand that ruined the illusion.

That was what the E-Bloc troopers, a team of two that emerged from inside the building, moving in synch, were looking at as they approached, the first round of bullets ringing out and chipping wood off the stall to his right. Viable cover was truly only a few feet away, but with guns trained on him and bullets flying, it seemed an impossible distance.

The difficulty of the task suddenly seemed even more dire when he noticed the body of the dark eyed Union operative sprawled among the dead in the middle of the street.

The flimsy stall wouldn't hold up for long under bullets of such high caliber, probably not even one of the cheap parked cars. On the next volley of shots, a bullet stung his leg, just barely deflected to the side by his armor. It was not a direct hit—but the round packed enough punch that he still went to his knees from the impact, positive he'd cracked a rib beneath the protective layer of fabric and Kevlar. Hayden felt the whipping air of more projectiles sliding pasts him, probably finding another target in the frantic civilians still trapped in the crossfire throughout the fish market.

He knelt, keeping his head beneath the topmost part of the stall's narrow counter, and sat the kid on the ground beside him. He wore two layers of the armor, a shirt and jacket combo, which made it easier to hide the shape of the gun beneath his clothing. Stripping off his jacket, Hayden wrapped the too-large piece of fabric around the boy's shoulders, before picking him up once more, and trying to figure out which direction was most likely to lead them to better cover and least likely to end up with Hayden's brains spilling out onto the sidewalk. If the kid wasn't already in danger of suffering from lasting trauma, a sight like that would certainly guarantee it. Picking out a low rock wall several stalls down, Hayden readied his gun and prepared himself to run.

He'd just jolted into position when one of the Union Americana operatives, the woman with red hair, planted herself in his path. Her back stayed to Hayden, her scavenged E-Bloc assault rifle pointing outwards, still firing at the E-Bloc troopers who were, to Hayden's eyes, much closer than they had been several moments prior.

"On me, slinger," she snapped, without daring to look back to see if he'd heard, and began moving across the market place. Behind Hayden, the E-Bloc troopers and Akiaten still fought, their furious exchanges punctuated by Laine's attacks as she now worked to extract herself from the core of the conflict.

In front of him, the operative kept firing as well, taking down one of the two E-Bloc troopers. She was cursing loud enough that Hayden could hear it over the noise bouncing from one building to the next, echoing off the water in the distance.

Suddenly, an Akiaten turned his fire on them from their vulnerable side. The man had come from out of nowhere, but thanks to Hayden's target finder and quick trigger finger several rounds found their mark.

The unexpected battle damage spoiled the Akiaten's aim and his shots went wide giving the redhead the chance she needed to plant a three-round burst of bullets in his chest. The Akiaten, from what Hayden could see, had no armor unless it was disguised in a similar manner to his own. The Akiaten dropped as the operative drove two more bursts into his torso. Hayden saw blood misting from the exit wounds on the other side of him when he fell.

The kid still wasn't looking, his head buried in the slinger's chest. Hayden was glad of it, following the operative as she led them to the mouth of a forgotten alley and herded him inside.

The operative did turn back then, long enough to check that the back of the alley wasn't a dead end and to look for possible assailants in its shadowed corners. Seeing nothing, she adjusted her hands on her gun and gave Hayden and the boy a smirk that meant to reassure.

Hayden looked behind her as Laine swept past the mouth of the alley with blood streaked across her face and a blade in her hands instead of a gun. The only thing he could guess was that most of the E-Bloc troopers were either dead, dying or fighting with the Akiaten in other parts of the marketplace. This gave Laine the chance for her relished close quarters fighting without much risk of being shot. He wondered if it was an Akiaten she had her sights set on or if there was simply a trooper lying somewhere, dying too slow for her taste. That woman had only one setting, and it was full throttle, doctor's and mechanic's advice be damned.

The redheaded operative had just turned back to the mouth of the alley, following Hayden's curious gaze, when the sound of shattering glass rang out behind them.

Neither of them had noticed the window that opened into the alley near its other end. It had exploded outward, a bloodied woman crashing through. Blood flowed thick and fast, unlike the still, drying streak he'd seen on Laine's face. Hayden could see that it came from her scalp, leaving a trail of wet, matted hair in its wake, but he could not see how deep it was, how deadly.

He lowered the boy to the ground and still keeping hold of his hand, started toward the limp body in the dirt. A few steps closer and he could see the rapid, shallow rise and fall of her chest.

"Cole?"

His name echoed after him, the operative's tone losing patience. She was probably pissed that his comparative inexperience with actual combat had forced her to separate from the alpha augment, not that being near her would be any safer if today was any indication.

"She's got major blood loss," he called back, as he knelt to examine her closely.

The operative neared the alley's mouth again, positioning herself in front of it and angling her body in the same direction that Laine had run. The sounds of fighting seeming to carry away from their current position, as if the roiling firefight had moved into another part of the neighborhood.

"Do you plan on starting a rescue station?" She looked back once more, looking from the boy to the injured woman.

Hayden snorted in nervous amusement but decided not to waste his time on a comeback. Not only would it distract the operative further from whatever target she was firing at, but he was feeling more stressed than petty. Still keeping the boy within arm's length, Hayden let himself look at the woman beneath all the blood. Dark hair, around his own age maybe, though it was hard to tell with all the blood. Her eyes were closed, tight, as if against the pain. He only knew basic first aid, knew that her pulse was too weak and too fast when he pressed two fingers to her neck. The wound on her scalp was not the only source of the blood, and there was a lot.

One hand was held tight to her abdomen and the blood that leaked out from between her slender fingers was thick and dark and showed no signs of stopping.

Fuck.

For a moment, man and boy both stared at the blood with hollow eyes.

A shadow shifted to Hayden's left, crossing the alley at the other end, shoulders hunched and breathing panicked. Just another frightened civilian trying to escape the gunfire, but the operator couldn't very well turn her eyes from the chaos of the marketplace, it would be just the opportunity the soldiers from either side would need to shoot her in the back, and the boy was too small and too scared to do much of anything. Hayden needed another pair of hands.

"Hey!" he barked at the man, forcing his voice out louder than he would have otherwise, channeling Captain Mitchell in the field. He was one of the few people Hayden knew who could control a room of rowdy operators with an authoritative elevation of his voice. The hunched figure paused and Hayden could see eyes shining in their direction.

"Help us," he continued, looking down at the woman and hoping the man tracked his meaning.

It was only when the man came closer that Hayden was able to glance up and get a real look at him.

An older man with wild eyes loomed over him, his clothing dirty, and in some areas worn ragged; the mismatched shoes on his feet told Hayden that he was homeless. His hair was matted and on the long side, mostly gray, though there was a wealth of dark brown still visible in his beard and a few streaks above his ears.

He knelt next to Hayden, watching where Hayden's hands were pressed tightly over the woman's. Hayden had not yet gotten a look at the wound, not even sure what had caused it, glass from the window or a stray bullet. Maybe not a stray bullet at all, observed a voice in Hayden's head, one that he chose to ignore even if it had a point. It was a night for ignoring good sense apparently.

The man was looking at Hayden, eyes narrowing as he took in his clothing. While perhaps not recognizable as bullet-proof, it was obviously well made, tailored to fit Hayden and no one else. The gun on the ground beside him was high-dollar as well. It was plain that Hayden didn't fit belong in this part of the city. The man was no doubt wondering what his part in this was, if he had, in some small way, contributed to the fate of the woman under his hands.

Hayden was wondering something similar, though he didn't let it show on his face. Deciding not to give the man the chance to ask too many questions, Hayden spoke as soon as he recognized the old man's expression.

"There's a medkit on the inside pocket of the jacket. The one the kid has on," he said, inclining his head toward the boy, who had taken the break in action as an opportunity to sit down in the dirt, both hands over his ears to drown out the popping gunfire.

The old man shuffled over to the boy and coaxed him out the jacket, saying something to him softly in Tagalog, the local language of the Philippines, that the child seemed to hear easily enough through the thin but stout armor. The kid looked slightly less terrified after hearing it.

It didn't take the man long to puzzle out exactly where the kit was. Hayden heard the rustle of fabric, the shuffling steps, and the man was again next to him, this time holding the kit in one gnarled hand.

At the front of the alley, the operator was now actively exchanging fire with someone. She wasn't pushing Hayden to move, either so focused on the fight that she'd forgotten about him, or perhaps had called for an emergency extraction and was waiting for a fire team to shoot its way to them.

The old man jumped at the fresh, close burst of noise, but Hayden was desensitized to sudden loudness, however close it sounded.

The kit came with instructions, and although it had been awhile since Hayden worked with it in the field, this was not his first time. He'd never used the kit on another person, but he had used it once to patch a bullet wound in his shoulder several years back. An earlier hit had already cracked the armor he wore and on the second hit, the bullet had barreled right through and into his bone. They'd dug it out back at HQ and fixed him up properly, but the joint still ached when it grew cold. Thankfully though, that was never much of an issue in New LA.

Hayden directed the man as best he could with his hands still splayed across the woman's stomach, overlapping her own. Though he could see that they were strong and calloused, the felt on the frail side, as though he might make the bones crack if he pushed down too hard. They grew colder the longer his hands rested there.

The old man ripped open one of the vacuum-sealed bags within using his teeth. It contained a powdered clotting substance that sealed shut anything it contacted. It might not be the synth-flesh dispensers that were issued to the alpha augments, but it worked. It should slow the bleeding if not stop it, and help the blood to clot. Of course, there was still the risk that the woman was bleeding internally, but there was little anyone could do for that outside of a hospital.

Hayden waited until the man had the bag almost on top of the woman and tilted up before he moved his hands, prying off the woman's hands as well. Her muscles had locked there, rigid as a corpse though her chest was still moving and her blood was still pumping. It looked to be an exit wound, the bullet entering somewhere from behind and ripping her middle to shreds on its way out.

The man moved quick as Hayden had hoped he would, dumping the contents of the pack onto the wound. The two of them watched, shoulder to shoulder, as the blood stopped bubbling outward. The old man looked at Hayden with his brows lifted, clearly impressed with the quality of the kit.

With great care, they lifted her up just enough for the man to dab a bit more of the stuff on the small, neat entry wound just above her kidney. They still needed something to put pressure on the slice in her flesh though, something to hold it together until someone with actual medical training could give her a look.

The man removed a thin jacket and held it out to Hayden who ripped off the lower half of the jacket, tore it into strips, and hung what remained back around the kid's shoulders.

All the while the fighting continued, yet so focused were they on saving this stranger's life, Hayden barely noticed. He'd never saved a life before, now that he thought about it, and his hands suddenly did not feel so slow and encumbered attending her wounds as they usually did when not flying across a keyboard.

However separate the alley felt, they were only a few yards away from the fighting, and the thought of the boy catching a stray bullet made his stomach do something strange.

Between the Old man and Hayden, they managed to rip up enough of their clothing to bind up the worst of the woman's wounds. They worked, for the most part, without words passing between them. It would have been difficult to hear anyhow.

It was in the middle of this that Hayden noted the knife that hung from the woman's belt, red crusted on one edge. She had no gun that he could see, but he had little trouble picturing her holding one. Maybe that was his own preconception, foisting his own idea of the innocence of bystanders onto this wounded woman. No going back now though, he knew he wasn't leaving her to die alone in this alley.

When the work was done, the woman looked much the same as she had before they began, face slack and drained of color, everything below the wound wet and stained red, like the ground beneath her. It coated the knees of Hayden's pants where he had knelt in it while he worked. Her breathing seemed to him less rapid, though he wasn't entirely sure if that was a good sign or simply a sign of her strength fading away with her blood loss. Hayden had no way of knowing. He and the old man met eyes across the body.

"Thank you," Hayden said, "For the help. You should-" He was about to tell the man to go. Unlike the woman on the ground between them, the man was fully capable of running away, of finding cover that would shield him better than an alley that was open on both sides. He was even considering telling him to take the boy with him but hesitated around the words. The man seemed kind enough, but that didn't mean anything. Cliché and sexist as it was, Hayden would have felt better leaving him with a woman, or at least a man who didn't have the look of a street urchin.

His high-rise Union lifestyle was rearing its ugly head, the prejudices that he thought he'd resolved roaring back to the front of his mind. Socio-economic prejudice was more powerful than ethnic differences in this post-war corporate culture and the slinger had to fight hard to push it out of his mind. He resolved to look for the boy's parents himself once the fighting died down. He was sure there was a police station somewhere nearby that the kid could be left at if all else failed.

He didn't get a chance to finish thinking.

The boy tugged at his sleeve, as sharply as a child of that size could have managed. The sounds of battle grew louder, closer, echoing off the alley walls. At the mouth of the alley, the operative still stood like a sentry, spraying bullets in both directions. From her rate of fire, he knew that the massive ammo drum that fed the weapon would soon click empty.

Hayden couldn't see, the alley narrowed his view, cut it off from both sides. By the time he saw the E-Bloc troopers closing in, they were already firing their weapons, too close for the operative's armor to do anything more than yield to their fire.

The first several rounds were deflected or absorbed by the armor as they were meant to be. The next several made a different sound, blunt and hollow and wet, like the noise the redhead's corpse made as it smacked against the ground.

Hayden grabbed for his handgun, heard the boy and the old man scrambling backwards behind him.

Only one of the troopers bothered with advancing down the alleyway; a slinger without his rig at hand, an old man, and a young boy did not merit more than one gun.

And they were right.

Hayden's hand had just closed around the cold metal of the gun's grip when the trooper fired, a straightforward, dead on shot, impossible to miss.

Had Hayden been covered with the other layers, the one he had stripped off and wrapped the boy in, the material he'd butchered to the bind up the woman's wounds, the bullet might have scarcely left a mark. As it was, the bullet found his chest, would have found his heart had it pierced through, but the slinger's armored shirt was just strong enough to stop it. Even so, that black rushed into his vision.

He felt his finger squeeze the trigger as he faded, but had no way of knowing whether his bullet found its mark.

12

The dark eyed operative moved at Laine's back, as he had ever since she'd lifted him to his feet after he'd temporarily blacked out from the impact of several direct hits to his torso armor.

She had not worked with him before, though she knew his last name was Thompson. She had read his file but knew little about him aside from his qualifications. Such things were generally deemed non-requisite by the likes of the Captain when choosing his security cadre. He moved well with her, despite his labored breathing through multiple cracked ribs and possibly a fractured sternum, and they were as seamless as two satellites circling their prescribed routes.

It worked this way when experienced professionals conducted combat operations together. Even though they were only armed with sidearms which were now down to their last few bullets, they had fared incredibly better than her tactical analytics had predicted once the shooting started. Even without the number of enhancements and augments that Laine had herself, he was good. Perhaps, if they ever decided to send her out with backup again, she would request him. Assuming either of them survived the night.

An E-Bloc trooper accosting a huddled group of civilians near the targeted building took a bullet to the kneecap as Thompson found his range. The trooper screamed for a moment before Laine transfixed his throat with her telescoping blade, fully extended to rapier length.

Thompson grinned as he walked alongside her, in the way that pro operators did when they knew they were making the best out of a bad day, his gun angled toward their more exposed left flank, ready to shoot anything that appeared, civilian or no.

Laine stepped over the body of an old man next to his overturned cart, her boot barely skimming his splayed arm as she went. There was no room left for pity in her hollowed-out chest. It was better filled with other things, useful things, like tactical indifference and cold calculation.

The second operative, Kelso, was nowhere to be seen, and she could only assume that she was with Hayden, and hopefully somewhere safe. However much it would have rankled any operative to remove themselves from the fight, such personal sacrifices were often necessary.

It was more important to keep Hayden from the line of fire than to feel the gun heat up under her hands. Without Cole's skill, their whole operation would in jeopardy. They had Nibiru for backup and a whole team of slingers backed by Overdog at their disposal, sure, but even with their nearly perfect team, their careful lineup, they had nearly been defeated by Asia Prime in the datascape. If something tilted the balance in one direction or another, that would be the end of their operations in Manila. At the very least, it would be the end of their chances to find and harvest the pulse before the others. They'd be lucky to pull out of the project with the rest of their teams and troopers intact.

Laine remembered glimpsing her, the operative Kelso, weaving through the stalls with Hayden at her back, his movements curiously careful and slow. She hoped he wasn't injured, he'd already nearly killed himself in MassNet just several days prior. Another setback would be inconvenient.

The E-Bloc troopers outnumbered the Akiaten, though for E-Bloc this was still a somewhat small detachment, perhaps expecting to take out the building quickly without interference.

Laine wasn't sure how they had zeroed in on the same target, they could have been hacked or tagged, but she doubted that. As wild as their initial drone flight and resulting datascape conflict had been, Nibiru and Hayden both had been careful, same with the research hack that had brought them here. Their own, separate surveillance may have simply led them to the same conclusion.

E-Bloc had a small army of troops in Manila, and likely a comparable slinger cadre and support staff for all of it. Or maybe, despite the precautions they'd taken when traveling to the site, they'd been tailed. This may have been about disrupting Union Americana's operations as much as it was dealing a blow to the Akiaten. Perhaps Hirohito was out there somewhere and tipped off E-Bloc, as the Akiaten slinger would certainly not have allowed a safe house to be burned in the datascape without causing such a shit storm about it that the Union slingers wouldn't have picked up on the disturbance.

Prior to this point, there had only been a handful of real fights and most of those had been confined to the datascape or the outskirts of the city. It had been easy for the local government to play along, to accept the money they were slipped and keep quiet. Now, with this many bodies on their hands (and civilians at that) Laine wasn't sure how they could turn a blind eye, no matter how handsomely they were compensated. There would be elections eventually, and as she'd said before, the powerful were focused on staying powerful.

The remaining troopers had begun to withdraw from the building, having heard the rising chaos outside and perhaps seen the Akiaten arriving in more and more force through the cracked windows.

The battle, from Laine's perspective near the edges of the fighting, once she'd made her exit, was beginning to look more like an actual street war. The fish market had not been in good shape when they arrived, but now it looked like the war-torn neighborhoods of places like Stockholm and Paris.

Dust filled the air and her lungs as she breathed and smoke drifted toward the sky from above the target building, her sinus filters kept the worst of it from entering her system, but the scent and taste of it still stung her palate.

Something inside was burning, and likely the building would collapse soon were it not attended to. She counted a few dead E-Bloc troopers and an Akiaten just from where she stood and even more locals scattered around the area. This same snapshot was likely repeated many times over in a circle of carnage that was spreading across the neighborhood.

The remaining civilians stayed under cover, crouched behind walls and in alleys, while others took their chances and sprinted to the docks. The injured were everywhere, lying on the ground or dragging themselves along on it, eyes wide and often looking past their surroundings.

She thought that it should have bothered her.

It had seemed to bother Cole the second he realized that civilians weren't being spared from the carnage, but Laine had no such feelings. The bodies on the ground were just bodies, and the people still bleeding would be bodies soon enough.

If she were capable of being frightened, perhaps her own detachment would have frightened her. The only time in recent memory she'd come close to achieving real fear had been the previous day's close call with Hirohito, where she'd been inches from being fried by the same bullets that had killed the Akiaten she wanted so badly to fight one on one. Even that hadn't been fear, more a distant sort of concern that she had regarded with the same coldness as she did the bloody scene around her in the marketplace.

Laine watched, Thompson still close in the shadows opposite where she stood, as the two groups began to light into each other in earnest. With her visual enhancements turned low, she could barely make out the shape of him there, just a blurry silhouette tight against the wall.

He's good, she admitted again, though she would have liked more of a chance to see Kelso work as well.

This conflict was escalating into open war, and if that was how things were going to go she imagined that soon she'd be leading strike teams into the heart of E-Bloc and Asia Prime operations.

She turned her attention back to the fighting between the Akiaten and what remained of the E-Bloc troopers, taking note of their tactics. E-Bloc was textbook as always, but their movements were so perfectly coordinated and executed with such brutality that it nearly made up for the lack of adaptability. In her opinion though, the Akiaten had them beat, or they would very soon. Their movements were just as well coordinated as E-Bloc's and completed with the same level of skill and devotion, but there was an unpredictability that made their attacks nearly impossible to counter. It was what she imagined it might have looked like to witness one of the many skirmishes between the ancient soldiers of the Roman Legion as they occupied the tribal lands of equally fierce and unpredictable Pict and Celt barbarians during the Iron Age.

She allowed herself one small moment, to watch an Akiaten vault over a stall completely, and land with the muzzle of his gun drilling into the skull of his enemy. It was a pity she hadn't thought to take a capture of it. She would have liked to watch the soldier's eyes grow dull.

She would have liked that immensely.

With such low numbers, she and Thompson could not rejoin the fight. To draw attention to themselves would give away the fact that they were part of neither group and thus easily wiped out.

Laine caught the operative's attention and signaled that he should move out when she did, not daring to use their short wave comms for fear of the broadcast being picked up by hostile slingers that were probably lurking in CodeSource.

When the worst of the shooting drifted a bit further away, closer to the docks, the choppy gray water broken up by bullets that had lost their way, the operative moved with her, as seamlessly as he had done throughout the battle. They made their way back the way they'd come.

Laine didn't realize how far they'd traveled from where they'd initially left their vehicle until she saw the nearly fully set sun glinting off the armored hood at the very edge of her vision. This area had seen the worst of the trouble, but now that it was relatively empty of violence, the remaining civilians were beginning to trickle out of hiding places, walking among the bodies and those who were too injured to rise from the ground in search of familiar faces.

At the sight of Laine and the operative walking through them, still armed and, in Laine's case, streaked with the blood of those they had killed, they shied away, backing away from whatever task they were in the midst of and abandoning them in favor of their own safety.

Laine had no energy to project into a disarming smile. She knew by now that they tended to unnerve rather than reassure the non-augmented. She kept her face detached as she paused, the operative unconsciously moving to protect her back as she did so.

This was the area in which she'd last seen Hayden, and, not seeing him in plain sight, she quickly pulled up her HUD and set his tracker to activate. They were all of them fitted with one nearly the second they signed their contract with Union Americana. They were meant to be turned on when you couldn't be located when something had gone wrong, when an operative or their corpse needed to be retrieved. She knew though, that they were just as often used when the corporation needed to track the movements of a certain employee who just wasn't quite trusted to complete the job as told. Flight-risks or traitors. Hayden was neither, as far as Laine was concerned.

By now, both she and he were well-known for their breaking of protocols, so neither bothered to attempt to baffle their own trackers, but, he may have been injured in the fighting or gotten turned around in the chaos if his own HUD had gone on the fritz. There was also the possibility that he'd been snatched and that was what made her chest feel oddly tight, especially when her search yielded nothing. She set the tracker to reboot, but a minute later (longer than it needed) there was still no response, no moving red signal to track on the virtual map.

Even if he was dead, there should have been a residual signal. That was how they recovered bodies in the field. It wasn't always possible, sure, but the corporation liked to pull it off whenever they could. It looked good to the folks at home, their devotion to their employees and their families. Their commitment to providing them with closure.

The tracker had been destroyed or disabled by someone who knew what a tracker was and how it worked.

A top tier slinger would be worth something.

They wouldn't have killed him, not E-Bloc nor the Akiaten, not if they had any idea who he was and what made him valuable.

Laine banished that sort of thinking, the hopeful sort. However much Hayden was worth to the Union, it would better for all of them if he was dead. If someone had realized his worth and taken him, to be interrogated for information on their corporation's workings or else used for their own means, then he was as good as dead anyway. If that were the case, then his eventual death would be prolonged and likely painful.

Despite all the evidence to the contrary, Laine found herself looking at the faces of the bodies she passed, much like the civilians, fingers crossed that she wouldn't trip over Hayden's corpse.

"Nothing?" the operative asked as they walked.

Laine shook her head. "Not on Cole. Not even residual signal." She adjusted the specs on the search. "I'll see if there's any sign of our fourth team member." Her voice came out steady, as though this wasn't a disaster. Laine was good at that. Indifference was one of the things at which she excelled.

This search came out better, revealing a fading signal just a few alleys down from where they had left the car. Laine linked their displays, allowing the operative to see what she did.

"There," she said, and together, they went.

The found the redhead at the mouth of the alley, her armor riddled with holes. It was designed to hold up against the toughest of penetrating rounds, but if you aim for the same spot too many times in a row, there's only so much it can take before the integrity weakens and it cracks, however strong it was originally. Each small crack made it more likely to give way. Her chest was in such horrid shape that it looked caved in, white slice of ribs exposed to the elements. At least she had not died alone, judging from the handful of E-Bloc troopers who lay dead in the street nearby, and with their own weapon turned upon them no less.

Laine wanted a capture of this as well, but operatives were trained to notice things, even those less skilled than Laine, and she was sure that her partner would notice and remark on it. That was why she preferred solo missions, no one to horrify with her brutality and no one to slow her down. No one to lose either. That was a plus.

Laine searched the surrounding area, walked to the end of the alley and back again, taking note of the broken window, the drying puddle of rust red on the ground, missing the body that went along with it. Not Hayden's blood. Her enhanced senses, cranked up as she knelt next to the puddle, told her that. Her last glimpse of Cole had been with Kelso leading him to cover, and she had little doubt that they were still together when the operative died.

The blood on the ground could have been E-Bloc, a trooper that ambushed them and perhaps, killed the operative as he was dying himself. With the broken window's position in relation to the blood, however, it seemed unlikely.

Laine could picture Hayden staying in the danger zone for the sake of a whimpering civilian. She could picture it easily, even if the man himself would have insisted till he was out of breath that he was not. However good a slinger he was, his part in the deaths of others had always made him just uncomfortable enough that she was sure it was listed in his files somewhere as a possible liability.

"Laine?" the operative said, his voice the precursor to a loud explosion at the west end of the market where the fighting had picked up as they moved out.

He was right. They had to pull out. Cole or no.

"One second," she said, quickly taking note of their coordinates, saving it to the same file in her HUD that she used for all taken field notes. When it was finished, she gave Kelso's corpse a nod and they walked from the alley. Someone would be back for the body if at all possible, when things calmed down, assuming it had not been recovered by the enemy. It was funny to her, always had been, that it was someone's job to retrieve dead things and bring them home.

The car felt small, the metal too close around her, the air hot and stuffy. They were careful not to draw any more attention as they climbed in, Laine in the driver's seat even though she felt too twitchy for it. She hoped having something to focus on, to wrap her trigger finger around, might quell the urge to leave the vehicle where it sat and track down the rest of the fighting. Her role in the battle aside, she badly wanted to kill someone.

Before she drove away, she sent notification of the failed excursion through the van's encrypted network, sent in a preliminary report and a low priority extraction request for the operative's body.

She reported Hayden as missing.

Her eyes scanned over the ruins of the market, the Akiaten and E-Bloc soldiers grinding each other to bits in the distance. She would have liked to fight them for longer. She was still owed her one on one contest of skill.

Laine turned the key in the ignition and turned her face toward the operative still holding his gun in the passenger seat. Both of them looked at the empty back seat bench.

"Standard defiance pattern, my perfect ass," Laine quipped bitterly.

She clenched her jaw and drove.

That tight feeling in her chest persisted. If her slinger wasn't already dead, in all probability he soon would be.

She wondered what Hayden's body would sound like when it hit the ground.

If someone would be there to capture it and remember.

Also by Sean-Michael Argo

Beautiful Resistance
Defiance Pattern
Opposition Shift
Significant Contact

Extinction Fleet
Space Marine Ajax
Space Marine Loki
Space Marine Apocalypse

Necrospace
Salvage Marines

Starwing Elite
Attack Ships
Ghost Fleet
Alpha Lance

Standalone
War Machines
DinoMechs: Battle Force Jurassic

Also by Sarah Stone

Beautiful Resistance
Defiance Pattern
Opposition Shift
Significant Contact

Standalone
War Machines

.